SEPTEMBER
17

SEPTEMBER 17

A Novel

Amanda West Lewis

Red Deer Press

Published in Canada by Red Deer Press
195 Allstate Parkway, Markham
ON, L3R 4T8
www.reddeerpress.com
Published in the U.S. by Red Deer Press
311 Washington Street, Brighton,
Massachusetts 02135
Edited for the Press by Peter Carver
Cover image courtesy of [COVER STOCK SOURCE HERE]
Text and cover design by Daniel Choi

We acknowledge with thanks the Canada Council for the Arts, and the Ontario Arts Council for their support of our publishing program. We acknowledge the financial support of the Government of Canada through the Canada Book Fund (CBF) for our publishing activities.

Library and Archives Canada Cataloguing in Publication
Lewis, Amanda West, author
September 17 / Amanda West Lewis.
ISBN 978-0-88995-507-3 (pbk.)
1. City of Benares (Ship)--Juvenile fiction. I. Title.
PS8623.E96448S47 2013   jC813'.6   C2013-904216-4
Publisher Cataloging-in-Publication Data (U.S.)
Lewis, Amanda West.
September 17 / Amanda West Lewis.
[320] p. : cm.
Summary: In September 1940, a luxury liner named The City of Benares is chosen to bring ninety British children to safety in Canada, but disaster occurs when the Benares is torpedoed by a German U-boat and sinks in just half an hour, with tragic results for the children. This gripping novel tells the true story of the catastrophe and the few children who survived.
ISBN-13: 978-0-88995-507-3 (pbk.)
1. City of Benares (Ship) – Juvenile fiction. 2. World War, 1939-1945 – Children – Great Britain – Juvenile fiction. 3. World War, 1939-1945 – Evacuation of civilians – Great Britain – Juvenile fiction. I. Title. II. September seventh.
[Fic] dc23   PZ7.L4957Se 2013

Printed and bound in Canada by Friesens

This book is dedicated to the children.

We need to decide that we will not go to war, whatever reason is conjured up by the politicians or the media, because war in our time is always indiscriminate, a war against innocents, a war against children.

—Howard Zinn, Historian and Author, from *The Progressive*, November 2001

I dream of giving birth to a child who will ask, "Mother, what was war?"

—Eve Merriam, poet, playwright, director

During the 1930s, Germany built up its army and passed laws restricting the rights of its citizens. The world watched nervously as the German army took over the neighbouring countries of Austria and Czechoslovakia. When they invaded Poland on August 31, 1939, Great Britain and France issued an ultimatum, demanding they withdraw. On September 3, 1939, when Germany failed to leave Poland, Great Britain and France declared war.

British and French troops tried to stop Germany's invasion of Norway, the Netherlands, Belgium, and Luxemburg, but one by one these countries fell. Then German forces invaded France, and on June 25, 1940, forced it to surrender. Anyone who resisted was killed. All Jewish people were deported, and their lands and possessions taken by the Germans. Many thousands of people died in the fighting.

British forces retreated to England. Bombing intensified. Germany's next aim was to take over England.

The English wanted to protect themselves and they

wanted to protect their children. They wanted to get their children away from the bombs, and away from the German invaders.

As more bombs fell, children were sent as far away from danger as possible. Thousands went to live with host families in the countryside. More than one hundred thousand children went to live on farms in Wales. The Children's Overseas Reception Board (CORB) was set up by the government to resettle English children in Canada, South Africa, Australia, and New Zealand. And so, a massive evacuation plan began to move children away from the war, to save their lives by moving them across the ocean to safety.

PART I

Chapter One

A heavy clod of wet earth fell on Ken's head. His hands began to shake.

It wasn't the hideous and sickening lurch of the ground. It wasn't the overwhelming, deafening crash. It wasn't even the thought of death. No, it was the idea of being buried alive that most terrified Ken.

He hunched on the ground under the arches of the train tracks of the Wembley Park Station. He listened to the distant drip of water, smelled the dank cool air coming from the tunnel. They said it was safe, but he couldn't stop imagining the bricks cracking, crumbling, and crashing down on top of him. He could taste the dirt, feel his crumpled arms beneath the tons of rubble, his open eyes seeing nothing, his thin voice reaching no one. He was pinned where no one would ever find him again, until bulldozers rebuilding the station overturned bits of his skeleton.

With every air raid, Ken pleaded with his father to let him stay in the flat. "If the flat gets hit, I'd still have a chance of escape," he'd say. "It's only wood and plaster. It's not like bricks and train tracks crashing down on you." Last week, when Mark's building was hit, his sisters had survived with hardly a scratch. Even Mark looked peaceful. Ken saw him as they lifted the broken boards off his body. There was hardly any blood.

"No, Ken, you can't stay here," said his father. "You've got to come with me and Mollie and your stepmum. We've got to stay together."

Ken didn't remember anything about his real mother. But he'd only been a year old when she died. His father had married his stepmother a year later. His stepsister Mollie would be nine in November.

Things had been all right for a while—when his father was working. But his father was having a hard time keeping a job. Ken didn't know what was wrong, but he hadn't had steady work for four years. Ken couldn't remember the last time his father had smiled. He spent most days sitting in his armchair yelling about the government and the price of a bit of tobacco.

Now, with the war, things were harder than ever. There were no jobs, and food was rationed. They had a real egg on Fridays, but mostly it was egg powder, chips, and day-old bread. Beetroot sandwiches were considered a treat, but Ken hated them. He got used to feeling hungry most of the time.

All his stepmother ever talked about was money. Ken and Mollie did whatever they could to bring in a bit extra. He had his early-morning paper route, and Mollie got a few farthings now and then when she cleaned the cages of the neighbour's rabbits. But it was never enough. "We could rent out your room for a quid a week," his stepmum railed. "We could get a decent bit of meat for Sundays with that, we could." Ken and Mollie shared a room, but his stepmother thought Mollie should move into the little box room down the hall. Ken wasn't sure where she thought he should move.

He watched a long-legged spider work its way down the brick archway in front of him. If they had a Morrison shelter at home, he could stay in there during the raids. Some of his friends had Morrison shelters right in their living rooms. Andy's had been set up just like a dining table. "When a raid's on, Mum just lifts the tablecloth and we go right in," he'd told Ken. Ken thought that it looked like a big cage. It would be awful to be squashed up in a cage with Mollie and his father and stepmum. But when Andy's house was hit, the whole front wall had fallen right on top of the shelter and Andy and his family were fine. They just opened the cage and walked out.

Since the beginning of September, Ken had spent most

nights—some days as well—under the Wembley Park Station. The government said stations were the safest places, unless you had a Morrison shelter, or a cellar, or an Anderson shelter in your backyard. But Ken's family didn't have a cellar or a backyard, and they were waiting still for their Morrison shelter kit to arrive.

"Soon," his father said. "The government's sending them out in alphabetical order. 'Sparks' is second half of the alphabet. 'Til then, we're together, in the arches, under the tracks."

They'd been there since teatime, listening to the drone of engines, the scream of fire engines in the distance. It had been a beautiful warm day, the kind of day Ken loved to spend poking around the factories or on the towpath of the canal. He was good at spotting things, and he often found little bits of metal and tinfoil that he donated to the war effort.

Now it was dusk and night was coming on. The sun was setting. He could see a glow in the distance.

But wasn't it in the wrong direction? The sun didn't set in the east, did it?

"East London's on fire," said his father, reading his mind.

Ken tried to concentrate on his drawing. He'd found a piece of shirt cardboard in the rubbish bin outside the flat—it had a bit of a grease stain along one side, but it was still perfectly good—and he was drawing to keep his mind off the bombing raid. His plane silhouettes were laid out in front of him and he was tracing the outline of a Hawker Hurricane. Even if it got completely dark, he'd still keep drawing. He could see the plane in his mind. That was all that mattered.

"Come on, Jerry!" Terry was striding through the tunnel, punching the air with his fist. "We're ready for ya! *Tat-a-tat-a-tat-tat!*" There were about twenty people under the arches. Neighbours, mostly. Terry went to Ken's school, but he was two years younger so Ken didn't spend much time with him.

Everyone froze as the sound of planes thundered directly above them. Ken held his breath and stared at his drawing. There was a brief silence, then a huge explosion, and a handful of stones fell from the archway. Ken covered his cardboard protectively and tried to ignore the world.

"Hey, Ken!" shouted Terry. "Do you think that one hit the school? Or maybe it was your precious library!"

The Wembley library felt like Ken's second home. He sat there for hours copying photographs of airplanes and war ships, reading and re-reading every newspaper he could get his hands on.

Ken wanted to be a war correspondent. He listened to all of the news broadcasts. He kept a tiny notebook and wrote down whatever he heard. He wrote down the direction that the planes came from during raids. He asked the boys in his class: could they guess how many had flown overhead?

He wanted to understand Mr. Churchill's strategy for fighting the Germans. But it seemed nothing could stop Hitler. When the reports from Dunkirk came on the radio, Ken couldn't make sense of what had happened. The British had evacuated forty thousand troops from under the noses of the Germans. People in Dover went in small fishing boats across the channel to France to help get the British troops home. But then they'd left France and it wasn't long before the French surrendered to the Germans. The French *surrendered*. It didn't seem possible. Now German troops were almost visible across the water, only twenty-one miles from English soil. They could practically swim over. They could invade any day.

A distant rumble like thunder shook the ground below him. Ken looked up at his stepmother. She was knitting— mitts, he thought—and Mollie's head was resting in her lap. He imagined water flooding through the tunnel with a boatload of Germans cresting a wave and opening fire on them.

By the time the all-clear sounded, it was almost dawn. They'd been there more than ten hours. The sun was starting to rise, as it should, in the east. A peaceful Sunday morning. Mollie was fast asleep. Ken offered to carry her, fireman style, up the dingy stairs and through the dark streets to their flat.

The air on the street was heavy with the smell of cordite.

His gas mask in its cardboard box bumped at his side. But he felt relief, the sensation of being physically lighter that he always felt on coming out from under the arches.

He barely noticed Mollie's weight on this back, but he couldn't see where he was going very well. He rounded the corner and smashed into Mrs. Hodgson. She was standing stock still staring straight ahead.

"Oh, dear God," his stepmum said quietly. Ken looked ahead. He could see a space in the row of houses, like a gap when a tooth falls out. The space where the Hodgsons lived.

"Ken," said his father quietly, "you take Mollie home. Your stepmum and I will see what's to do." He watched as his father strode grimly ahead, toward the blank space that seemed to suck all light and sound out of the air.

Later that day, it was Ken's job to play with Giles and Graham. He was supposed to keep them occupied while the Hodgsons searched the rubble for anything useful.

"Have you anything t'eat?" Giles' freckles were covered with a fine layer of soot. His eyes were wide as he looked up from the floor in the front room where he and Graham were scooting Ken's dinky cars around the chair legs.

Ken was in the kitchen spreading thin smears of Marmite on pieces of stale toast when Jenny stepped in through the back door. She had a small smudge of dirt on her nose, but she looked strangely glamorous.

"Looks like we've picked out everything we can safely get. The warden says we're not to move anything else. Too dangerous."

Ken felt embarrassed by her serious dark eyes. He had a sudden flash of a memory from a couple of years ago—before the war, at any rate—of seeing her laughing as she boarded a tram, with dancing shoes hooked over her fingers.

"Did you get much?" The vision of that space without a house was burned into Ken's mind.

"Naw. It's all buried too deep. The hard part is not having nappies or milk for the baby. I fancy you could hear him screaming all the way over here."

Suddenly, Giles came bounding into the kitchen. "I'm stayin' here, Jenny. They got Marmite!" Crumbs flew every which way as he jammed the toast into his mouth and tore off back to the lounge.

Ken looked down at the empty plate. He didn't know what to say to this girl whose life had just been shattered. He cleared his throat and tried to make his voice sound normal. "Do you want a cup of tea?"

"Naw, that's all right, Ken. I've got to collect up the boys."

"Where'll you go?"

"We're not sure yet. Back to the archway tonight. My aunt Is says she can take in two or three of us. We've a gran in Slough. She's just got a bedsit, but still one of us might go there." She smiled sadly and shrugged her shoulders.

"Nine's too many for anyone to take all together."

Ken let her words sink in. "At least no one was hurt," he added hopefully.

"Oh, I'm sure it will all work out. There's many folk have to deal with far worse. Graham! Giles!" She called out in her singsong voice.

"Not goin'!" Giles shouted down the hall. Ken heard a squeal and a thump. Graham dragged his brother toward them. The five-year-old was squirming and thrashing.

"No! I wanna stay. Wanna play cars! Don't wanna go t'shelter!"

Graham kept a tight grip on Giles as he handed Ken the two cars. "Here, Ken. Thanks for lettin' us play." Ken looked at the cars balancing on his open palm. His Cooper Bristol racing car. His Vauxhall Saloon. They suddenly looked very small.

"That's okay, Graham," he said. "You can keep them to play with in the shelter, if you like."

Giles suddenly stopped squirming and grabbed the racing car. "This one's mine!" but Jenny caught his eye and he quickly added, "Thanks."

Ken handed the Vauxhall to Graham. "Ta, Ken."

"Race you to the house. I mean, to the rubble," Graham shouted over his shoulder to Giles as he took off through the backdoor.

"No fair!" screamed Giles, running after him.

"Thanks, Ken. Those cars will keep them going for hours," said Jenny as she turned to go.

"That's all right. I've kind of outgrown dinky cars."

"Still, it means a lot," she said.

Ken had cleared up the toast crumbs and was drawing at the table when Mollie came in with his father and stepmother.

"I can't think what that family'll do. Whatever were they thinkin', havin' all those children? They can't live under the arches forever—there's no toilet for one, and no kettle for another. And no one here's got extra." She rounded on Ken. "You sittin' here drawin', while rest of us is tryin' to find a few things for those poor souls. Haven't you got tea on yet?"

By the next day, Ken had forgotten completely about the Hodgsons. He went off to school as usual, only to find that the east end of the building had been hit in the raid. School was cancelled. There'd be no school for the rest of the week. Next week he'd get bussed to Wembley Manor School.

When Ken arrived home early he could tell he was interrupting a conversation that he wasn't supposed to hear.

"It'll be good for him," his stepmother was saying. "Make a man of him. We can move Mollie to the box room, and have a spare room to rent out. Think on it—an extra quid a week! And my sister will get money from the government to look after him, which is more than we get."

Suddenly, Ken's father saw him and looked up angrily. "What'd you do? Why're you home?"

"School's closed. Hit by a bomb."

As Ken looked at his father he realized that he looked more sad than angry. "Well, that's that, then," he said.

"What's what?" asked Ken. He sensed something, but he didn't know what. He felt his stomach flop over. His father looked at his stepmother. "You're a smart lad, Ken. You should go to a good school. And I want you to survive this war."

"Kenneth," said his stepmother, "You need to pack to go to Canada."

Ken felt cold all over, as though his body was filled with ice water. His ears were ringing. He couldn't make the words make sense.

"You're to stay with my sister in a place called Edmonton," she continued. "The government will pay for your trip over. You're to gather your things and be ready by tomorrow mornin'. Here's the list."

A list? Canada? Away from home, from Mollie, from everything he knew? Away from the war? Tomorrow? It didn't make sense. How on earth could they afford to send him to Canada, when there wasn't enough money for a proper meal? His stepmother must be trying to trick him.

"Where's the money coming from?" he asked warily.

"Don't need money," said his stepmother. "I just told you—government pays for it all. Aren't you the lucky so-and-so!"

"But Canada's across the ocean. How am I supposed get there?"

"By boat, of course. Do you think the government would make you walk?" His stepmother laughed.

"But a boat'll take a long time! How long'll I stay? And when do I come back?"

"You'll come back when the war's over, Ken," said his father softly. "No one knows how long that'll be. Two, maybe three years."

He stared at his father. His head was spinning. Three years? They were sending him away for three years? In three years he'd be sixteen.

He'd always dreamed about sailing. Now he could go on a real ship. A ship to Canada. He'd be away from bombs. He'd be away from the archway. He felt as though his brain was on fire.

"Where am I sailing from? What ship? How big is it? Will I get to work on the decks? Do you know—"

"Do I look like a bloomin' encyclopedia?" said his stepmother. "All I know is you've got to be ready to go. We got the letter this mornin'. And you're not to tell anyone where you're goin'. Says so in the letter. They could change their minds if you tell."

"But they must've said something about the name of the ship. Otherwise how do I know which one to get on?" Ken was afraid that his stepmum hadn't paid attention to the details.

"I just told you. It's a secret. We're to take you to Euston station tomorrow and they'll put you on a train. That's all I know. So gather up those things on the list, and write your name on all of your clothes, just like it says there. And mind you tidy your room before you go."

He looked at the clock on the mantel. It was only ten in the morning. The library would just be opening. If he hurried, he could get there and find out everything he could about Canada and Edmonton. He could look through shipping reports and try to figure out which ship it might be, and which route they might take.

He raced out the door. He was going on a ship. Across the ocean. To start a new life.

TUESDAY, SEPTEMBER 10, 1940

The next morning, Ken's stepmother made him breakfast as usual—a bit of watery porridge—but she put a drizzle of treacle on top for a special treat. Mollie wanted some too, so Ken shared a bit of his.

"Where're you goin' then, Ken?" she asked. He'd managed to keep it a secret all night, but it might be years before he saw Mollie again. He couldn't lie to her.

"I'm going on a boat, Mollie. Going to Canada."

"What? Why? Can I go too?" Mollie turned to her mother. "Can I go with Ken to Canada, Mum?"

"No, Mollie, I need you here with me to help out. Ken's older. And your aunt Phyllis can only take the one of you. It's so Ken can go to a good school. His school got bombed."

Ken knew his stepmother was running through as many reasons as she could, without saying any of the real reasons. He knew it would be easier for them all if he wasn't there. They could rent out the room and have a bit more to eat. Besides, he *was* older. This was *his* adventure.

"Aunt Phyllis lives in a place called Edmonton, Mollie. That's where I'm going. I'll see snow igloos and Eskimos and Indians and beavers, and I promise I'll write you all about them. And you can write and tell me what's happening here." Ken felt a lump in his throat. "Then when the war is over, I'll be back to see you."

"Well, that's all right then," said Mollie. She was distracted by the treacle stuck to her teeth. "I'm goin' to be late for school." She picked up her gas mask and slung it over her shoulder. "Tala, now, Ken. I'll see you when you get back."

She doesn't understand, Ken thought. *I'm going away to sea, and in three years, when I am sixteen, I can join the navy as a cadet and stay away at sea forever*. But all he said was, "Tala Mollie. You mind yourself."

After Mollie left, Ken's father came into the room carrying an overcoat.

"See here, Ken. I know it's a bit big for you now, but I suspect you might do a bit of growin' over the next while. I think you might need it to keep you warm, what with the snow and all. So you put it on, and you wear it always. You'll be glad for it."

"You look after that coat, mind, Ken. Don't you go losin' it," said his stepmother.

Ken stared at the overcoat. He knew it was his father's good coat, the one that he kept at the back of the closet for special. He put it on. The arms came down over his hands, and the bottom was below his knees. His legs looked skinny in his short pants, sticking out below the coat.

"Thank you very much." He looked at his father. "Thank you very much, sir," he added.

Chapter   Two

When the bombing started, Bess's school was turned into a fire hall for the auxiliary fire service. From the window in her bedroom, she could see the schoolyard filled with black London taxis, requisitioned for the war effort, trailing long fire hoses. Strong young men cleaned equipment and practiced fire drills in the warm sunshine.

Whenever she could, Bess went over to the school's lunchroom to play piano and talk to the volunteer firefighters. Many of them were young, not much older than Bess. The war was definitely the most exciting thing that had ever happened to her. The bombs seemed a small price to pay for the adventure.

But she was supposed to move to the country in the autumn, to go to St. Alban's with the rest of her school. She was determined not to go.

"What's the point?" she argued with her mother. "School will be only half days, because we have to share the rooms with a whole other school. I'll be stuck out in the country with nothing to do."

"Well, you could always do some extra studying," her mother said with a smile.

"I can do that here," Bess replied. "I've got all of the textbooks and I can do the work in half the time here. Besides, if I stay here I can help with the war effort. I can help make sandbags."

"Bess, your father and I are concerned about you falling behind," said her mother. "You're almost fifteen. Even with the war on, we want you to be thinking about college, about your future."

"I *am* thinking about my future," Bess replied. "I get straight As and I can do that by studying hard here, at home." Bess knew it was important to her parents that she get a good education. Her father had run a tobacco shop, but when she was eight he'd had an accident. He didn't talk about it much, but the only job he could get after that was as a school caretaker. That's when they'd moved to Kentish Town. He always said if he'd had a better education, he could have gotten a better job and they could have stayed in Stepney. Her mother had been to university and had taught for a while, but of course she didn't work after Bess was born. Bess knew they wanted her to be a teacher.

It wasn't hard for her to be a good student, but she'd never fit in at school. She was big for her age, and she got teased about her thick glasses. Her father often brought books home for her to read and they'd talk about them over tea. Just before the schools were shut down, he'd brought home the one by Mr. Hitler, *Mein Kampf*. "It will help you to understand what is going on," her father had said.

Bess looked at her mother and took a deep breath. "I've already asked the head mistress."

"What? Bess, how could you ask Mrs. Stevenson without consulting us first?"

"Because I wanted to make sure that it would work. She said that as long as I get all of my work done and I hand it in on time, she'll make sure it gets marked. I can mail it to her. She said she understood my wanting to stay and help look after Louis. She thought I was being very altruistic."

Bess loved the way the word sounded when Mrs. Stevenson said it. She could almost believe that she actually was doing this for Louis, although she knew that her brother didn't really need to be looked after. He was nine, after all. But her mother liked her to keep Louis out of trouble.

"Besides," continued Bess, "They're moving the school to the country because of the bombing raids. I'd rather be here with you, being bombed, than stuck out in the country all alone, worrying about you."

For some reason, Bess wasn't frightened of the bombs.

Her family had an Anderson shelter in the back garden and she actually liked the evenings where they crouched together as a family, playing Snap, trying to distract each other from the sounds around them. It was like a big metal cave and she felt safe there with her family.

The day after a raid held a special kind of magic for her. She loved looking out on the changed landscape of Kentish Town, seeing buildings with no front on them. Just like giant dollhouses. She imagined the lives of the people who had lived in them. If the buildings weren't cordoned off for rescue or recovery, she and Louis would spend hours sifting through the rubble—he, looking for shrapnel; she, for bits of jewellery.

She looked at her mother and smiled her best "devoted daughter" smile. She'd spent the day at the fire hall with her new friend Gareth. He'd noticed the blue glass brooch she'd found last week. He said it matched her eyes.

"I'll speak with your father tonight," her mother said, a slow grin creeping into the corners of her mouth. "Perhaps it would be best if you were here with us, where we can keep an eye on you."

FRIDAY, AUGUST 30, 1940

It had been a beautiful summer, and Bess had spent most days at the fire hall, playing piano for the volunteer firefighters. She'd just gotten a round of applause for playing "A Nightingale Sang in Berkeley Square," when Gareth burst through the door.

"Wish me luck as you wave me goodbye!" he sang, as he marched through the room. Bess laughed.

"I don't know if it's proper for you to be laughing at Aircraftman Williams, my girl!"

Bess's mouth fell open. "You've enlisted? But you can't. You're not old enough yet!" Her heart was pounding.

"I'll be eighteen in two weeks, and they said that it would take that long to get me papers, so that's all right. Royal Air Force, here I come!"

A whoop went up in the hall. The other men crowded around. They shook Gareth's hand and clapped him on the back.

"You're leaving?" Bess's voice sounded weak amidst all of the congratulations.

"Of course!" said Gareth, "I've got to do my duty to God and the King. Besides, this way I get to see the world. I'll fight those Jerries and get this war over with. I'll come back a hero."

"But what about your little brother? He's going to miss you terribly." Bess knew that Gareth's parents had both died in a bombing raid and that he was looking after his brother full time.

"Ah, that's all part of the plan, my girl. He's headed off to Canada!"

"But how can he do that? Where did you get the money?" It was all she could do not to burst into tears.

Gareth laughed his big booming laugh. "The government's sent him. For free! They're sending anyone who wants to go. Well, anyone between five and fifteen. You get to go to Canada or New Zealand, Australia or South Africa. It's brilliant!"

"For free?" asked Bess.

"Absolutely! It's a government plan called CORB— Children's Overseas Reception Board. He's on a boat called the *Volendam*. He sailed for Canada yesterday. We've got a cousin in a place called Banff, so he gets to go and live with her in the Rocky Mountains."

The Rockies. Bess had seen pictures of those mountains in her geography class. Canada was huge. It was a place for adventures and romance. She'd read a book about an orphan on an island in Canada, a girl who was really smart and clever, who wasn't very pretty but who went away to university and fell in love.

Gareth had enlisted. He'd be gone in two weeks. She looked around at the younger fire fighters. She knew that they, too, would probably sign up as soon as they could. So many had left already.

Being left behind was awful. Going to Canada sounded like it might be a pretty exciting adventure.

For the past two nights, the skies had filled with German bombers. Many of the stores in the high street had been destroyed and today her mother had come back from shopping without any supplies. She looked tense and careworn. Bess waited until they were washing up after their tea of watery stew and stale bread.

"Mum, maybe it's not so safe for us here after all. The bombing is getting really bad. And I know with rationing, it's getting hard to feed us all." Bess carefully dried her plate. Her mother was silent.

"Louis and I are having a hard time with our school work, and I'm worried about what will happen if it gets worse." Bess knew that if she included Louis in the plan, there was a much better chance that her mother would say yes.

"I know, love," said her mother sadly. "We may have to think about sending you to St. Albans after all."

"Well," said Bess, "if we need to go away, and if you really want Louis and me to be safe and to get a good education, why don't you send us to Canada?"

Her mother put down the pot she was scrubbing and gripped the edge of the sink. The words Bess had practiced flew out of her mouth.

"There are really good schools in Canada, and people there who want to look after us. Lots of people have volunteered to take in English children to get us away from the bombs and the Germans." Safety and education. She knew that's what mattered to her parents. "There are no bombs. Canada's perfect," pleaded Bess.

"Canada is on the other side of the world," said her mother sternly. "It is a terribly dangerous trip. Why, just three days ago the SS *Volendam* was torpedoed trying to make that crossing."

"Yes, I know," said Bess, "But no one was hurt. Everyone was rescued. The Royal Navy guarantees safety crossing the ocean. It says so right here in the paper." Gareth had given Bess a copy of the notice in the paper about the CORB plan.

"Bess, your father and I already know about this plan. We've actually talked it over a lot. I have an aunt in a place called Winnipeg who might take you in. But we aren't sure that we want you to leave. We know it's hard here, but people just have to stick out the tough times."

Her mother handed the pot to Bess to dry and continued. "The Queen has said that she and the princesses are staying here, even though many countries have offered them safe haven. They are setting a brave example."

"I don't want to set an example. I want to go to a good school and to learn about the world," Bess shot back.

"But, darling, no one knows how long the war will last. If you leave, you might be gone for years."

"And I would come back with a degree from university, just like you, Mum. I couldn't get that here, not if I have to live in the country and go to that pokey grammar school in St. Albans."

"Darling ..."

Bess threw down her teatowel. "If I stay here I may not die of a bomb, but I *will* die of boredom!" She stomped out of the room. She knew she was being hurtful and hideous but she wanted, desperately wanted, to get on with her life. At any cost.

MONDAY, SEPTEMBER 9, 1940

Bess had just sat down for breakfast when the postman arrived with a large manila envelope stamped *On His Majesty's Service*. She knew immediately what it was. She scooped up Louis and the two of them started to dance around the kitchen.

"When do we leave?"

"Where do we land?"

"Which suitcase can I take?"

"Can I take my Bulldog Drummond books?"

"Oh, can I take my *Anne of Ingleside*?"

"I'm taking my Hornby train set," insisted Louis.

"I'm not sure it will all fit into your suitcase," said their mother.

"I'm sure I can fit some of it in my case," said Bess. She'd have agreed to anything, anything, just to make sure that they could go.

"I, for one, will be glad to get you noisy lot out of here," said her father.

Bess plopped herself in her father's lap and laughed as she put her glasses on his nose.

"Oh, Daddy, you don't mean that. You'll miss us. But we will write every day and we'll tell you stories about the mountains." Bess could see herself by a window with a view of snow-capped peaks in the distance.

"And I'll shoot a bear and send it back to you to make a coat, so you'll be warm for the winter!" said Louis proudly.

"No, thank you!" said their mother. "If I hear anything about you and bears I will get you back here on the next boat, war or no war! Now, finish up your breakfast. We've got a lot to do. You're to be at Euston station tomorrow morning.

Tomorrow! Bess knew it would happen quickly, if it happened at all. She felt her heart pound. Tomorrow her new life would begin.

The regulations said that the suitcases had to be small: sixteen by eighteen inches. And the lists were very specific: one cardigan or woollen jumper, one woollen dress or skirt and jumper, two pairs of stockings, six handkerchiefs, and on and on. Bess's list was longer than Louis' and included sanitary pads and a sewing kit. In the end, there was no room for the Hornby train set in either of their tiny suitcases.

"Well, I won't go," Louis stamped, clutching his beloved train engine.

Bess knew that if Louis made a fuss now, she'd never get to Canada.

"Louis, I think it would be all right to carry the engine. It doesn't have to go in the suitcase. And then, when we get to Winnipeg, I'll use some of the money that I've saved to buy you a new Canadian train."

Louis eyed her suspiciously. "Really? Promise? Cross your heart?" Bess was all right as a big sister, but she wasn't usually this nice.

"Of course, I promise. And your English train cars will be right here, safe and sound, waiting for you to get back."

Bess had sewn their names and their CORB number onto each item of clothing. She insisted on packing her worn old green dressing gown, even though her mother had used up all of their clothing coupons to buy her a brand-new one. "I love the old one. It reminds me of home," she said. She knew that she'd hurt her mother's feelings, but she'd make up for it, somehow. Later.

Bess longed to tell people where she was going, but the letter from the government was very clear. *Loose lips sink ships. Ears are everywhere.* It was vital that the enemy didn't know when ships were leaving, where they were leaving from, or where they were bound.

They tried to make everything look as normal as possible, as though they were still busy with the war effort. The army had dumped a huge pile of sand beside their house and Bess and Louis spent the late afternoon with their neighbours filling sandbags. The full bags were going to be distributed throughout London to shore up walls and windows. But all Bess could think about was the trip ahead.

That night there was an air raid. They sat together as a family, as usual, in the Anderson shelter in the backyard. They played Snap, the same as every other night.

"Cocoa, Bess?" Her mother began pouring the hot liquid from the flask. Cocoa was a special treat. Her mother must have bartered something valuable to get some. Suddenly, Bess felt a pang of sadness. She imagined her mother and father sitting alone in the shelter and felt her eyes sting. But then she made herself think about the boat and the adventure ahead. After the war she'd come back to Kentish Town. She'd have a university degree and she'd get a job teaching. After the war.

TUESDAY, SEPTEMBER 10, 1940

Euston station wasn't far from Kentish Town, but her father took the morning off work to travel with them on the bus. Louis fidgeted as he tried to juggle his suitcase, gas mask, and train engine. Bess had her father's copy of *Freedom and*

Culture under her arm, a book he loved. He had pressed it into her hands last night.

"I'm not going to make a big speech," he had said, "You're a good girl, and you've got a brain in your head. Use it wisely."

Bess was also carrying a packet of sardine and cheese sandwiches that her mother had given them for the train ride. They were made with "National Loaf," which her mother made with old flour, water, and yeast. It was dry and hard and went stale really quickly. Bess knew that her mother had saved up ration cards to be able to give them both sardine and cheese sandwiches. She knew that she should be grateful. But she couldn't wait to get to Canada, where she hoped there'd be no food rationing.

There were lots of children at Euston station. A CORB official was checking off each one and giving them a name tag to wear. A boy in an oversized coat, with skinny pale legs jutting out beneath, was standing just ahead of them. "Kenneth John Sparks," he said clearly. "Ken," he corrected.

The woman checked his name off on the list. "Right, Ken. Here's your name tag. Have you got your case? And your gas mask? Good lad. Just go on through to platform 13 there, and find a seat on the train with the other children. Next!"

"Elizabeth Walder, but everyone calls me Bess. And this is my brother Louis." Bess watched the woman check off their names. "We've our cases and gas masks here."

"And I can see you've got a fine Hornby engine," the woman said, smiling down at Louis. "That's grand. Say your goodbyes now and head on over to platform 13." Bess moved aside as a girl with two sisters and two brothers took her place. "Gussie Grimmond," Bess heard her say, "An' 'ere's Connie, Violet, Eddie, an' our Lenny." Gussie looked to be a couple of years younger than Bess. Bess was glad she didn't have to look after so many siblings.

Bess turned to her parents. Her father was pretending to take the engine away from Louis, who was squealing. Her mother's face was flushed.

"Now you take care of your brother," said her mum quietly. "I know he can be a naughty boy, but I want you to look after him."

Then her mother hugged her and whispered in her ear, "You grow up and be a good girl."

Her father gave her a quick peck on the cheek, "I'll always love you."

Louis had wriggled through the barrier and headed onto the platform along with a couple of the other boys. He had a huge grin on his face as Bess caught up to him. Then they were inside the train, poking their heads through an open window.

Just then the stationmaster's whistle sounded outside on the platform. "Last call for Liverpool!" he shouted. "All aboard!"

Louis waved wildly to their parents. "Don't forget to

look after the rest of my train set!" Louis called out. Bess's heart lurched as the train began to move. She waved as she watched her mother and father recede into the distance. They were off.

Chapter Three

"Liverpool!"

Bess turned away from the window. She was in a compartment with Louis and Ken, the boy in the long overcoat.

"That means we'll go through the middle of the Atlantic, almost straight across to Halifax, I'll bet," Ken said. "Maybe we'll be on a destroyer!"

Bess watched as he took a notebook and maps out of his pocket. "We'll go right past where the SS *Volendam* was sunk last week. Maybe we'll see some action! We'll blow some Germans outta the water!"

Louis' eyes widened. "Do you think they'll show us how to aim the torpedoes?" he asked.

Just then a little boy with thick blond hair came flying into their compartment.

"Alan, get back here!"

An older boy, about nine, bumped his way into the compartment, balancing two suitcases, his gas mask, and a full paper bag.

Little Alan dove under Bess's seat and started squirming along the floor.

"Hey, Derek!" Alan shouted from under the seats. "You should come under here! The Germans won't find us here. And there's a whole bunch of chewing gum!"

"Don't eat it!" said Derek plunking himself down into the seat beside Ken.

"Little brothers can be such a pain," he said. He pushed back a lock of hair from his eyes. "How'm I supposed to look after him all the way to Canada?" He looked over at Louis. "Hey, what's that? Is that a Hornby engine?! Can I see?"

Louis held out the engine for inspection.

"Wow, that's a beaut!" said Derek. "Our mum told us there'd be lots of new toys for us in Canada, and we didn't need to bring any with us." He looked down, slyly. "But I couldn't leave this behind."

Derek dug into his pocket and pulled out a tiny Supermarine Spitfire.

"Ho-ly!" exclaimed Ken and Louis at the same time.

"De-rick! Mum said you had to leave that behind!" Little Alan squeezed beside Louis. "What am I gonna play with?"

"How about this?" Derek dug deep into his pocket again. He held out a tiny tank.

"My tank! You brought my tank!" Alan snatched up the dinky toy and began whizzing it around the floor of the compartment.

Bess watched as Ken pulled out his map to show Louis and Derek the route he thought they'd take. *Louis is making new friends already*, she thought. *He'll be all right on his own for a bit.*

"Louis, I am just going up to the next compartment," she said, picking up the book from her father, *Freedom and Culture*. It didn't look very exciting, but she thought it would help to pass the time. Louis nodded vaguely as he listened to Ken explaining the convoy routes.

Bess walked into the corridor and down to the next compartment. She saw Gussie Grimmond with her brothers and sisters. The two little girls had cut out paper dolls from magazines. Their brothers were playing with cars on the floor. Gussie was re-packing their suitcases. Bess thought she'd check to see if the next compartment was a bit quieter. She walked further down the corridor and saw a small pale boy sitting all by himself, clutching a brown paper bag. He looked to be a couple of years younger than Louis. She sat down quietly beside him.

"Hello." The boy stared down at his paper bag.

"My name's Bess. What's yours?"

"John. John Snoad."

"Nice to meet you, John."

John continued to keep his eyes on the bag in his lap.

"What have got in your bag, John?"

"A photo of me mum. An' a piece of bread an' butter," John muttered softly.

Bess realized that she hadn't brought a picture of her parents. She wondered if that was something she should have done. For Louis.

"Would you like to show me the photo, John?" she asked. John shook his head slowly.

"Have you ever gone on a boat before? It'll be my first time. I'm pretty excited."

"Don't want to go on a boat. Want to go home." John said quietly.

The train, which had been moving very slowly, stopped. John looked up at Bess. She stood and looked out the window. Suddenly, another train thundered past them, so close that Bess instinctively jumped back as it barrelled along. She saw a blur of soldiers' uniforms as the passing train shot past the window.

When their train started up again, it moved at a snail's pace. John seemed determined not to talk, so Bess tried to read. But her book was heavy going and she was distracted by the noise of the children in the other compartments. The train swayed from side to side. Little John's head drooped down and rested on her arm as he fell asleep. Bess let the movement of the train lull her into a soft dream, a dream of boats and sailors ...

Bess's head jolted sideways and hit the window as the

train jerked to a stop. "Ow!" John's wide eyes stared at her.

"Everybody out. Quick now." A conductor was striding quickly through the corridor. "Bring your gas masks, children."

"Are we at Liverpool?" asked Bess as the conductor moved past her.

"No, this is Ellesmere Port. It's an air raid. Got to get you lot into the shelter."

John was still clutching his paper bag. He picked up his gas mask.

"You head out with the others, John. I've got to check on my brother," said Bess.

She pushed past a line of children to get back to the compartment where she'd left Louis and her gas mask. She shouldn't have left it behind. That was sloppy. Louis was waiting for her at the door. Ken was beside him, with a map open. "We're really close to Liverpool," he said. Derek and Alan were scrambling under the seats of the compartment. "I'm sure I left it around here somewhere," whimpered Alan.

Children were streaming out the doors of the train toward the station. Bess saw the Grimmond children stumble out together.

"Stop pushin', Vi!"

"Let go o' me!"

"I'm tellin' ..."

"Gussie, Lenny pinched me!"

They made their way into the cellar of the train station. By the time they got settled, Bess felt rubbed raw. It wasn't like going into the shelter at home—this was a terrifying chaos of unfamiliar voices and fear. There were about forty children, many quite young and rambunctious like Alan and Lenny. Bess sat in the dark of the shelter, sharing the last of her sardine sandwich with a little blonde girl named Joyce and her large teddy bear named Winchell. Together they listened for the distant whistle and whine of bombs. Louis sat on the floor beside her, tracing circles in the dirt with his Hornby engine. Ken had perched himself on a bench in the far corner. She saw John Snoad staring mournfully at his paper bag.

Bess fought down feelings of homesickness. She just wanted to be on the ship and headed safely out to sea.

After twenty minutes the all-clear sounded and they were herded back onto the train. By the time they arrived at the Liverpool Central Station it was late afternoon. Bess stood on the platform with all of the other evacuees, unsure and tentative. The ocean was nowhere to be seen.

A young woman with short-cropped hair, wearing a bright blue Women's Royal Navy Service uniform, strode up, clapped her hands, and asked everyone for attention. She was only a couple of years older than Bess and she, too, wore large glasses.

"Righto, lovely to see you boys and girls. My name is Wren

Wallis. If you'll just follow me. You are to change trains here to go to Fazakerley for the night."

The children looked at the woman, confused. Louis whispered to Bess, "Where's the ocean, Bessie? Where's the ship?"

"Excuse me, Miss—I mean Wren Wallis," said Bess in a clear voice, "But what is Fazakerley? Is it the ship?"

"Oh, goodness, no. You won't be going to the ship for two days," said Wren Wallis cheerfully. There were groans from some of the children, and Bess heard at least one little girl start to cry.

"Now, now, there's no problem. You are going to stay at the Children's Homes in Fazakerley. It's not too far really. Twenty minutes by train and then a bit of a walk at the other end. It's an orphanage, and there's a school right beside. They've made room for you and the others," said the woman.

There was a lot of talk, and a bit of grumbling at this news. "Not to worry," she added, above the chatter. "They've got a good tea on for you lot." She turned to Bess. "Let's gather up some of these little ones and get them there as soon as we can."

The thought of tea cheered Bess. Little Joyce tugged at her sleeve. "Did she say tea? Do you think there'll be a bicky?"

Bess smiled down at her. "There might be." She took the

girl's small hand in hers as they started to walk through the station to the local trains.

"Do you think they might have choc'late? I haven't had a choc'late bicky since they started dropping bombs," said Joyce cheerfully. Bess tried to remember the last time she'd had a chocolate biscuit. She wondered if they had chocolate biscuits in Canada.

They settled themselves onto the small local train. Joyce continued to hold Bess's hand for the whole ride to the Fazakerley station.

"Mum told Jack he had to look after me," said Joyce, "But Winchell and I'd rather stay with you." She hugged her teddy bear closer.

Bess saw Joyce's brother Jack eying Louis' train engine. She could hear him telling Louis all about his new boots. "My father bought them special, for our trip. He was a soldier in the Great War and he really wanted us to go to Canada for this war."

In Fazakerley, they left the station and began a walk along tree-lined streets. The late afternoon light had lengthened into long shadows as the air began to get cool. Joyce started to sniffle. "I'm tired," she sobbed. "I want to go home."

"It's only just a bit farther, Joyce. Then we'll have tea. And maybe biscuits." Bess was feeling pretty tired herself. It had been a long day. She could only imagine how exhausted this tiny girl felt. "Here, why don't I give you and Winchell a piggyback?" Bess hoisted Joyce onto her back.

Louis came charging up with Jack and another boy in tow. "Bessie, this is Fred. He knows everything there is to know about sailing ships!"

Fred grinned at Bess. His blond hair was sticking up in clumps. "Well, my father and uncles are all seamen. Even my grandfather was in the navy, during the Boer War, so it's all we ever talk about at home. I can't wait to be on our own ship!"

By the time they got to Sherwoods Lane Girls' School, Bess could barely remember starting out on the journey that morning. Had it really been only one day? But when she walked into the large assembly hall and saw the long tables set out with plates of potted meat sandwiches and bowls of jelly for dessert, her exhaustion evaporated.

"Choc'late bickies!" squealed Joyce as she scrambled down from Bess's back and ran to her brother at one of the tables. The room was filled with the sound of laughter as everyone began to devour the food.

As they ate, more children arrived. Bess realized that their group from Euston station was only one of a number that would be staying in Fazakerley. The assembly hall was packed tight and the sound was almost deafening.

At the end of the meal a woman with a round friendly face stood up to get everyone's attention.

"Hello, boys and girls. My name is Miss Abraham. I am

headmistress here at Sherwoods Lane Girls' School and I would like to welcome you all. We are very pleased to have you here with us before you head out on your voyage. I hope you enjoyed your tea?"

A loud cheer went up, and Miss Abraham beamed.

"I'm so glad. We all want you to enjoy your short stay with us. We've got lots of activities planned, and we've set up beds for you in the orphanage cottages. But first, we need to divide you into groups. To do that, I'd like to introduce your head escort, Miss Marjorie Day. She is in charge of getting you safely to Canada."

A large, dark-haired woman with a broad smile strode to the front of the room and held up several sheets of foolscap paper. "Well, aren't we all on a wonderful adventure! Here we are in Liverpool and in two days' time we'll be on a ship to take us all to Canada." At this a huge cheer went up, but Bess saw John Snoad's face crumple.

"As Miss Abraham said, we're going to put you into groups. Each group will have its own escort who will look after you in the cottages," continued Miss Day. "All of the boys are going to sleep in one cottage and all of the girls in another. That means that you may be separated from your brother or sister. But don't worry—you will still see each other during the day. Now, listen closely for your name."

Bess listened as Miss Day called the names out. Louis went with an escort named Michael Rennie. Alan and Derek, the boys they'd met on the train, were also in his group. Michael was easily one of the handsomest young men that Bess had ever seen. He had a big ball with him and immediately began a game of keep-away with the boys. Ken, the boy with the maps, and Joyce's brother Jack went with a group led by a priest named Reverend King. John Snoad trailed behind them.

Joyce was called to go into a group with an escort named Mary Cornish. "But I want to stay with you," Joyce cried, clutching Bess's hand.

"It's all right," said Bess. "We'll still be together in the cottage. Look, I've saved you one of my biscuits, to have at bedtime."

Miss Cornish gently took Joyce's hand from Bess. Beside her was another small girl, with eyes that flashed under a dark fringe of hair.

"Joyce, this is Marion. Her brother Rex is in your brother Jack's group. We're going to have a sing-along once we have our beds arranged, and I need both of you to help me think of some songs."

Joyce looked shyly at Marion. "This is Winchell," she said, introducing her teddy bear. She broke her biscuit and offered half to Marion. "Do you know 'On the Good Ship Lollipop?'" Marion asked, as Miss Cornish led them away.

Bess, Gussie, and her sisters Connie and Violet were all put into escort Maud Hillman's group. Miss Hillman had a soft face—what Bess's mum called doughy. Her dark brown hair was coiled into a tight bun on the back of her head. She led them out to a long, low cottage with thin wooden walls. The floor was covered with rows of white rectangles, each about four feet long and two feet wide.

"What are those?" asked Gussie.

"Why, those are palliasses, Gussie," said Miss Hillman. Gussie looked at her blankly. "Your beds."

Bess eyed the thin pallets suspiciously. "I know they're a bit flat," said Miss Hillman. "They're only filled with a bit of sawdust. We'll have better ones on the ship, I dare say, but we'll have to make do with these for a couple of nights." Bess doubted she'd get a very good night's sleep lying on the floor with all of these strangers.

"Well, it'll be better than the floor of the tube station," said Connie.

"Yeah," said Violet. "We've been sleeping in the station for two days 'cause our 'ouse got blown up."

"And 'cause there's ten of us, there was no place to put us so we get to go to Canada! Right, Gussie?"

Suddenly, a girl burst through the door and rushed up to Miss Hillman. "Excuse me. Are you Miss Hillman? My name is Beth. Beth Cummings. I think I am supposed to be in your group. I accidentally went off with Miss Day but she said I am to be here with you."

"Oh yes, hello, Beth. Good. I wondered where you were." Miss Hillman checked the name off on her list. "Don't let anyone know I've started out on my first day by losing you!

Let's make sure we all stick together from here on in."

Beth laughed and turned around to look at the rest of the group. Bess caught her eye. "Is Beth short for Elizabeth?" she asked.

"Yes," said Beth. "What's your name?"

"Well, my name's Elizabeth, too, but everyone calls me Bess."

"Elizabeth and Elizabeth. Good Queen Bess, and Princess Elizabeth. A queen and a princess!" Beth laughed.

Bess saw a book in Beth's hand. Beth handed it to her. *Anne of Ingleside*. "It's by a Canadian," Beth said. "It's the sequel to *Anne of Green Gables*. It just came out."

"I know," said Bess, "I loved it better than anything."

When it was time to go to bed, Bess and Beth bunked down side by side on their thin palliasses. Beth told Bess that she lived in Liverpool. Her home had very nearly been blown up several times in the last few weeks. She had come to Fazakerley on a bus with a woman from CORB.

"I'm really glad to be leaving the bombs, but I'm worried about my mum," she confided. "It's been just me and my mum. My dad died last year." Beth spoke quickly, half whispering in the dark beside Bess. Bess couldn't help thinking about her own parents. She was glad they were together. She couldn't imagine how hard it would be for her mum if she were alone.

"My brother Geoff is in the army fighting somewhere in the desert and my other brother Tom is in Canada training to be a pilot," continued Beth. "He says there's trees everywhere in Canada."

"And mountains, too," said Bess. "I've seen pictures of the Rockies. They're beautiful!"

"I'm going to a place called Toronto to stay with my aunt and uncle. But I really want to go to Prince Edward Island, just like Anne of Green Gables," said Beth.

"Me, too!" said Bess. "Especially if there are boys there like Gilbert Blythe!"

Beth laughed. "My mum says that the only reason she can bear to send me away is the hope that at least *one* of us will come out of the war alive. But the way I see it, I get to have an adventure!"

"I'm glad we can have an adventure together, Princess Elizabeth!" laughed Bess.

Chapter Four

Sonia stood on the newly built concrete breakers. She looked over the huge boulders to the sea beyond. She was straining her eyes, trying to see the coast of France.

There was no beach in Aldwick anymore. Last autumn, soldiers had taken away hundreds, probably thousands of truckloads of sand. Then they used tanks to move the boulders in place. Sonia knew that the sand was for sandbags to protect buildings from the bombs, but she hated that they'd taken it all away. It wasn't that she still made sand castles or anything like that. She was eleven. She didn't really like the feeling of sand between her toes. But she loved to look at the beach, her beach. Now it was gone. She wondered if they'd bring back all of the sand after the war was over.

It was all right for Barbara. Barbara was fourteen and

she was happy as long as she had a book to read. And her little brother Derek loved the war. He'd race outside when he heard planes in a dogfight. He'd wait to see where the losing plane spiraled down to earth, then bike over there as quickly as he could. Of course, he was really excited when it was a German plane that crashed. He came back with all sorts of gruesome stories—he'd seen a decapitated pilot once. Last week he'd been playing inside an old deserted tank when a Typhoon fighter plane used it for target practice. He'd almost been killed when the Typhoon strafed the tank with bullets. Sonia's mum had been really angry with him that day, but it didn't stop him from going back the next time he heard the bombers. He thought the war was a great game.

Their father worked in London and only came home on the weekends. He said the bombing was even worse there. But since June, when the Germans had taken over France, what they were all really scared of was the thought of the Germans invading England. They were just across the channel. On a clear day like today, Sonia was sure she could see France from Aldwick, although her mother had told her time and time again that was impossible. As she stood staring out over the concrete breakers, she imagined the German boats landing on her beach that wasn't a beach anymore.

Last Friday when Sonia's father got home, she overheard her mother's strained, frightened voice pleading with him to stay with them. "If the Germans invade England, Aldwick is probably one of the first places they'll land."

"You know I have to be in London to look after the business. Things don't stop just because there is a war on," he'd said.

FRIDAY, SEPTEMBER 6, 1940

Sonia's father arrived home early. He had three large new steamer trunks with him—and four first-class tickets.

Barbara was furious. "We're running away?"

"No," said her father patiently. "You are going to safety."

"It's wrong to leave. We should be staying here to help!" Barbara glared at their father.

"I want to stay here and fight the Jerries!" Derek was working himself up to a nine-year-old-sized tantrum.

"I want to stay here with all of my friends," cried Barbara.

Their father held Barbara in his eyes as he spoke.

"You are going on a huge luxury ship, converted for wartime use. You are going to Canada." He turned to Derek. "Derek, I am going to loan you my special suitcase. I can't go with you, so I need you to be the man of the family."

Derek's face relaxed into a grin. "To Canada? With the Eskimos?" he asked.

"I don't think there are any Eskimos with your cousins in Montreal, Derek, but you can look around when you get there."

"But—" Barbara began.

"Enough," said her father sternly. "I won't have your mother living through bombing raids, or worse, an invasion. It was hard enough surviving the Zeppelin attacks in the Great War. No one should have to face it again."

And so it was settled. They were leaving for Canada the next week. Sonia was sorry to leave her dog Mackie, but really excited at the idea of travelling across the ocean. She felt like she was going on holiday. A holiday to Canada.

WEDNESDAY, SEPTEMBER 11, 1940

Sonia wore her new camel-hair coat that they'd bought especially for the trip. Her trunk was filled with a new wardrobe of blouses, cardigans, skirts, and stockings, even new outfits for her doll Lolly. They had so many trunks and cases that they needed two porters to help at every stage of the journey.

The train to Liverpool kept stopping because of the air raids. By the time they arrived it was dark. Derek was whiney and annoying, and Barbara wasn't speaking to anyone. Sonia absentmindedly brushed all of the tangles out of Lolly's hair. She was bored and hungry when they finally got to the hotel.

But when they walked into the front door of the Adelphi Hotel, all of Sonia's exhaustion and bad temper vanished.

"Oh, Mummy, look!" A huge glass chandelier filled the centre of the spacious lobby. Sonia's eyes flitted around the room. Golden angel heads were carved on top of the frames of the blacked out windows. Marble inlays created delicate patterns on the floor.

"Good evening, Mrs. Bech. I am sure you are all tired from the journey. Can I arrange tea for you in the lounge while we take your trunks up to your rooms?" asked the hotel manager.

"Oh, yes, please!" Sonia burst out. Derek was already speeding his toy cars on the marble floor. Barbara was heading for a large armchair, clutching a book.

WWOOOOOOAAAAAAH. WWOOOOOOAAAAAHHHHH. Suddenly the air-raid siren sounded.

"*No!*" Sonia started to cry. "It isn't fair! I want to stay here in the lounge and have tea!"

"Sonia," said her mother sternly. "Pick up Lolly. Derek, gather up those cars. Now." Barbara had already changed her path to follow the hotel porter and all of the hotel guests down to the basement.

"But we just got here!" Sonia started to sob. She wanted to sit under the chandelier with Lolly, both of them in their new clothes.

"Sonia. Enough. They'll bring us tea in the shelter," her mother sighed. "And remember, this is why we are leaving."

The makeshift bomb shelter was adapted from the hotel's

Turkish bath deep underground. It was cavernous with tile benches along the walls and pointed archways leading off to other rooms. *At least it's roomier than our Anderson shelter back home,* thought Sonia grumpily.

"Look how fast my cars can go on these tiles!" shouted Derek happily. His whizzing sounds echoed off of the vast walls.

The hotel guests talked quietly until the bombs started in earnest. Then the noise became deafening. Sonia curled up beside her mother on the cool white tile bench. The porter had given them all tea in china cups, with little dry biscuits on the side. But Sonia left hers untouched. Derek stopped whizzing his cars. Barbara put down her book. Endless booming sounds echoed through the Turkish bath. *This stupid, stupid war,* Sonia thought, as she tried not to be afraid in the strange surroundings.

THURSDAY, SEPTEMBER 12, 1940

At breakfast, a large woman leaned over their table. "The tramway is at a standstill. And they aren't letting anyone drive into the town." Sonia was trying to eat her lumpy egg and toast fingers. Ever since they started using powdered eggs, Sonia hated breakfast.

"A bomb hit Liverpool Central Station, right where you came in yesterday. And there were six people killed in Edinburgh Street, just across from where my aunt May lives." The woman's loud voice jarred as it echoed through the dining room. "Mind you, she's already left for the countryside. But I just don't know how we'll get anywhere today. There are huge queues for the buses." The woman made a face as she bit into her eggs.

Sonia's mother nodded and smiled tensely. "Sonia, can you go and find Derek? Barbara, please double-check to make sure everything is packed up. We've got to be ready to go the minute the car gets here."

Sonia knew her mother had a way of getting what she wanted. While the rest of the city was at a standstill, the dust settling on the shattered streets, Sonia's mother guided them to a car, driven by a man with a small Royal Copenhagen logo on his uniform.

"It's a company car. From our Liverpool branch," said her mother. "Your father arranged for it."

The driver circled around destroyed streets and bombed-out buildings, through a maze of detours to get to the port and the Prince's Landing pier. Everywhere Sonia looked, there were huge piles of bricks and rubble, with bits of metal poking out every which way. *Those piles used to be shops and people's homes*, she thought. The whole city seemed to be a huge mound of destruction. This was a lot worse than Aldwick, she realized.

The car stopped. Sonia looked out. In front of them was a gangplank leading to a huge ship. Even though it was painted in camouflage colours, there was no mistaking the luxury liner for a warship. Black letters along the prow read: *City of Benares.*

Even Barbara was stunned. "That's our ship? It's enormous!"

Sonia thought the ship looked like something out of a picture book. She smiled as she walked up the gangplank. She imagined herself arriving in the colony and walking back down the gangplank in her new camel-hair coat.

Chapter Five

Ken's mind registered that he felt stiff and cold. He snapped his eyes open, alarmed at the unfamiliar surroundings. At home he always woke early, usually around five. It was his favourite part of the day. He loved the quiet and the chance to think. He'd lie still, listening to Mollie breathing across the room while his mind woke up. Then he'd pick up his notebook, pen, and torch, and snuggle under the blanket to write and draw.

But now the sound of sleeping boys all around him seemed incredibly loud. He couldn't imagine that he'd been able to sleep through the night with all of that breathing, snuffling, coughing, and murmuring going on. He realized he'd been dreaming. His hands were twitching on the controls of a Spitfire. He was trying to pull it out of a dive.

There was a high-pitched whine as the plane plummeted toward the ground ...

He listened to the sound of his own breathing. Instinctively, he reached under his head for his notebook. It was too dark to write, and he had no torch. But holding it felt good, familiar.

He wondered about Mollie. Had her bed already been moved into the tiny box room? Did she like being all alone, or did she miss him? *When it's light*, he thought, *I'll write to her.*

Little John Snoad was sniffling in the bed beside him. Ken had tried to talk to him last night. He'd tried to tell him a story about Canada and snow, but John had just cried harder. He'd cried so hard that he started coughing, and then he'd coughed so hard that he could barely breathe. Their escort, Reverend King, had taken him for a walk outside, in the dark. When they got back, the reverend was carrying the boy, who was asleep. Now here he was starting to wake up and crying already. It was going to be a long day.

"Hey, Ken. You 'wake?" Terry was on the other side of him. Ken had been surprised to find Terry on the trip. He couldn't imagine him on a destroyer. He wasn't the adventurous sort. And Ken wasn't really happy to have anyone he knew from Wembley here on his adventure. It seemed an amazing coincidence. But Terry was thrilled. The minute he'd seen Ken he'd latched onto him and followed him everywhere. Ken wished he could pretend to still be asleep.

"Ken?"

"Yeah."

"Wadda you think they'll give us for breckers? Will there be a bit o' egg?"

"Dunno. Mebbe."

"Is that John cryin' over there?"

"Yeah."

John's sobs got louder. Ken saw Reverend King's tall silhouette tiptoeing around the bodies on the floor as he worked his way to John's side. The sounds in the room grew as boys all around him began to wake up to the new day.

"Johnny, come back here!" a strained voice cut through the morning air. Johnny and his brother Bobby were in Ken's group. After yesterday's tea, they'd all spent a lot of the time hunting for Johnny. He'd eventually been found in the schoolyard, collecting early conkers that had fallen from the chestnut trees. He looked like he was heading out again.

"I don't want breakfast! I want to go home!" wailed John Snoad.

Ken found his pencil. He started to sketch the Spitfire from his dream. He drew it from the pilot's point of view, taking great care with the instrument panel, and even drew his own hands on the steering wheel. He let the drawing drown out John's tears, Terry's questions, Bobby's shouts.

Tomorrow, he'd be on the boat. He just had to be patient.

The adventure was so close he could almost touch it. Soon.

After a breakfast of bread, powdered egg, and porridge, Ken's group went to one of the school's classrooms. Reverend King had a stack of pictures of Canada. Ken had seen most of the pictures already, but he loved looking at the fields of golden wheat and the huge trees coming out of rocks by the side of lakes. There didn't seem to be any people in Canada.

"I was born in Ontario," said the reverend in his harsh Canadian accent. "It's a province in the middle of the country."

"What's a province?" asked Terry.

"It's like a county, only a lot bigger. The whole of England would fit into this little part of the province of Ontario." Reverend King was pointing to a tiny part on the bottom of the map of Canada.

"That's impossible," laughed Bobby.

"Yeah," said Johnny, "England's huge! You just don't know."

"We'll be landing here," continued the reverend, "at the port of Halifax. And then we'll continue on to Montreal." He pointed to another dot on the map. "Depending on your final destination, you'll get off and take a train from either Halifax or Montreal."

"Will Johnny come with me?" asked Bobby.

"Brothers and sisters will be kept together as much as

possible," said Reverend King. "As long as we don't lose Johnny before we get there, I'm sure you'll be together," he laughed.

The door opened and Ken saw escort Michael Rennie surrounded by his group of boys.

"Enough school work for now, don't you think, reverend? It's a beautiful day and these boys need a good football game to stretch their legs after all of that travel yesterday."

"I'm Eddie," a little boy peered into Ken's face. "Are you gonna play? What's your team gonna be? We're th' Bolton Wanderers!"

"The field's perfect! We've already got our positions," said Louis. Ken saw that he was still carrying his train engine.

"Michael's got us training," said Derek. His brother Alan was jumping up and down with excitement.

Michael Rennie was the youngest of the escorts and with his tanned face and white Oxford sweater tied loosely around his neck, Ken thought he looked like a movie star. Clearly, his group idolized him.

"Come on then, boys," said the reverend. "Let's show them what you're made of!"

WOOOOOOOAAAAAHHHHH. WOOOOOOOOAAAAAHHHHHH. Suddenly, the too-familiar scream of an air-raid siren filled Ken's ears. He felt a brief moment of panic.

"All right, everyone, pick up your gas masks. We can get to the shelter through the back end of the school." Reverend King took John Snoad's hand. There was no sound of aircraft. Perhaps it was a false alarm. The corridor quickly filled as everyone calmly headed to the end of the building, to a narrow door surrounded by sandbags.

As Ken went underground, he eyed the wooden boards that held back the earth. Were they strong enough to withstand a hit? There were more sandbags here, and rough benches along the sides of the walls. He followed the reverend into one of the back rooms. More and more children crowded in. Ken felt his panic rising when suddenly the distant sound of the sirens was overpowered by a rich tenor voice.

> On the farm, every Friday
> On the farm, it's rabbit-pie day.
> So, every Friday that ever comes along,
> I get up early and sing this little song.

Michael Rennie smiled broadly as he sang. Soon everyone joined in.

> Run Adolf—run Adolf—Run! Run! Run!
> Run Adolf—run Adolf—Run! Run! Run!
> Bang! Bang! Bang! Bang!
> Goes the soldier's gun.
> Run, Adolf, run, Adolf, run.
> Run Adolf—run Adolf—Run! Run! Run!

Ken sang at the top of his lungs, working to push his fear down. He sang so hard that he almost drove away the recurring image of the boards above him shattering and the earth covering his mouth and nose.

When the all-clear sounded, Ken headed out to the playing field with the rest of the boys as though nothing had happened. He couldn't help looking up at the sky for bombers, but it was a clear blue day. A false alarm this time. Or perhaps someone else was hit, in some other town, somewhere close by.

Ken had just fallen asleep. It had been a fun day of football, with time to draw and write a letter to Mollie. They'd all been given medical exams and he'd been declared fit to travel. He'd gone to sleep happily tired.

WOOOOOOAAAAAHHHHH. WOOOOOOOAAAAAHHHHHH. The sound smashed into his brain.

"Everybody up! They're close! Grab your masks. Leave your shoes! Run!" Reverend King was herding the boys out of the cottage toward the air-raid shelter. He was half carrying, half dragging John who was screaming and coughing. Ken began to run across the damp night grass, crouching low as he'd been taught. The dark sky was lit by flashes of tracer fire from anti-aircraft guns. Fighter planes crisscrossed the sky. In the distance he could see flames bright against the moonlit night.

Moonlight. They'd be easy to spot as they ran; ninety

ragged children and ten adults, running across the open sports field. He ran faster. It had been bad in Wembley, but never this bad. He'd never had to run across an open field, with bombers directly overhead. He dove through the open door of the shelter, tripping over a tiny girl who was sitting in the doorway crying.

"Winchell! Did you bring Winchell? Where's Winchell?"

Miss Cornish, one of the other escorts, picked the girl up.

"It's all right, Joyce, your teddy will be fine. But we have to get into the shelter. Way in the back," she said, guiding Joyce in, away from the noise and the chaos.

Ken's brain was filled with the sound of the sirens, the heavy drone of plane engines, distant crashes as bombs hit their targets, and crying of children. The ground shook and a shower of dirt fell onto Ken's head. He fought the urge to scream. He couldn't make out any faces in the dark of the shelter, but he was aware of the crush of bodies. He heard others crying out around him, brothers and sisters trying to find each other, escorts looking for lost little ones.

"Ken! Is 'at you?" Terry's face swam into focus. "It's close, ain'it? Didja see the anti-aircraft fire?"

Ken nodded. He'd avoided Terry most of the day, but now he was glad for this friendly face, glad that Terry needed him. His heart was racing but his body felt calmer.

"Yeah," he said, "it was shooting at a Heinkel He11. Did you see the way the gunners on the German plane shot back? With machine guns at the back and front?" The plane's image was burned into Ken's brain. The more he talked, the calmer he felt. "That's how you know it was a Heinkel. Because of where the gunners were sitting. Also because of the way the nose is made. It looks like a greenhouse. It was probably heading for the port."

Then he had a sudden, horrifying thought. What if their ship got bombed in the port? The evacuation would be cancelled. He'd never get to sea, never get to Canada ...

THURSDAY, SEPTEMBER 12, 1940

After the terror of the night raid, Ken woke to bright sunshine and the thrill of adventure. Today was the day! They were finally packing up to leave the Children's Homes in Fazakerley and head to the docks. Ken wanted to make a good impression on the crewmen, so he slicked down his thick black hair and made sure that his coat buttons were shiny. He wished he could wear long trousers instead of his short school pants. He hated the way his skinny legs stuck out of the bottom of the long coat.

"All right," said Reverend King, "gather up your gas masks and your cases. There's a bus waiting to take us to the dock."

Ken started for the door, but slowed down when he saw little John sit down on his palliasse.

"Come on then, John. Today's the day!" For the first time since they'd arrived, John seemed happy. He finally wasn't crying.

"Bye then, Ken. Have a good time."

Ken stopped in his tracks.

"What?" said Ken. "Whadda you mean? Are you not coming to Canada, John?"

John's voice came out in a wheezy rasp.

"Nope. Nurse says I've got assmaticcold. They said they can't take anyone who's sick." Now he had a big smile on his face. "They're putting me back on the train this afternoon." He held up a paper bag. "And they've given me a sardine sandwich! Won't my mum be surprised when I walk in the door."

The sun shone brightly as they rode the bus down to the Mersey Estuary at the mouth of Liverpool Bay. Nothing had prepared Ken for how large and beautiful their ship was. It towered above them all, gleaming in the sunlight. He knew at a glance that it was not a destroyer. It was a luxury liner painted in camouflage colours. He wondered where it had sailed before the war, before all ships were taken over for the war effort.

"Holy moly!" said Terry beside him. "Who knew that war was going to be so much fun?"

Chapter Six

Bess started up the gangplank of *City of Benares* with Louis, who was juggling his train engine with his case and gas mask.

A brown-skinned man in a bright white turban and shiny black shoes that curled up at the toes stretched out his hand to help them aboard. "Please madam, welcome. Welcome, little sir. Welcome to you. Welcome to our ship."

A line of Indian men dressed in coloured turbans and light white cotton uniforms with ornate blue sashes at their waists all bowed as they stepped onto the deck of the ship.

Louis' eyes were wide as he turned to Bess. "It's like the *Arabian Nights!*"

"It's like a floating palace," Beth whispered behind them.

"Ah, memsahib," said one of the Indian men to Miss Hillman. "Please to follow me, memsahib."

Bess, Beth, and the other girls in their group followed Miss Hillman as the Indian man led them along the deck to a metal stairway. They walked down two levels, along a corridor to a series of cabin rooms with beautiful heavy wooden doors. One of the doors was open, and Bess saw a girl looking out a shiny brass porthole window. The girl had a huge smile on her face as she turned to Bess.

"Oh, hi!" she waved. "Are you going to be next door?"

"I think so," said Bess.

"Rosemary and I are in Miss Day's group. We're going to swap beds every other night. She gets the top bunk tonight, and I'll get it tomorrow. My name's Eleanor." There was another girl with long blond braids stretched out on the top bunk, her hands behind her head, grinning.

"I'm Bess. I'll visit later," she said, waving as she hurried to join up with the rest of her group.

Miss Hillman assigned Bess to a cabin with a girl named Patricia. Patricia was a bit younger than Bess, with dark curly hair and a sense of being in charge. She seemed to Bess to be immediately comfortable in their room.

"You could fit everything my family owns in this wardrobe!" said Patricia, striding over to open it. There were drawers along each side, and a pole to hang dresses.

"The royal tour will begin in ten minutes," said Miss Hillman. "Unpack your things, girls, and meet me up on deck."

Bess and Patricia carefully put their clothes away in the

wardrobe. "What about this?" she said to Patricia, holding up her gas mask. "Do you think we'll need them at sea?"

"We're supposed to keep them with us until we set sail," said Patricia knowledgeably. "I was on the *Volendam*, and that's what we were told there."

"You were on the *Volendam*?" said Bess. She remembered that Gareth's brother had been on the ship, that it had been torpedoed, but that everyone had been rescued.

"Yes!" said Patricia with pride. "After I got rescued they took me straight to Fazakerley. I didn't even go home."

"What? You've just gone from one ship to another?"

"Well, my home had been bombed out so there wasn't a home to go to." The girl shrugged her shoulders. "It's hard to imagine that I started off two weeks ago, and here I am, starting again. This ship is a lot bigger, though, and much prettier."

Bess picked up her gas mask. "I need to go and find my brother," she said. "I'll see you up on deck?"

"For sure!" said Patricia.

Bess went out into the corridor and poked her head into the cabin next door, where Beth was unpacking with Joan.

"Meet you on deck in ten minutes," she said as she set off to find Louis.

But after she'd turned several corners she soon realized that she wasn't sure which way to go. Just as she was thinking she might be lost, one of the Indian men appeared as if by magic.

"Is little madam lost?" he asked politely.

"I am trying to find my brother. I think his cabin is on the starboard side." She wasn't quite sure if that was the right word. Miss Hillman had said that the girls were on the port side, the side facing the port. She thought that the boys were probably on the other side, which she thought was called starboard.

"Yes, of course. Please to follow me." Bess followed the man as he turned and twisted though several corridors. She was soon completely disoriented.

"Excuse me," Bess started to speak to the man before she really knew how to ask her question. "Excuse me, but what am I to call you?"

"Ah, yes, little madam. I am Ramjam Buxoo. I am the serang on the ship. But you may call me boy."

"Boy?"

"You may call most of the lascars boy and they will answer to you. If boy is not their rank, they will still answer."

"Lascars?"

"We lascars are the crew who make the ship to run. We have come from our home in India with this ship, *City of Benares*. We help to cook, we serve, we grease the engine, we scrub and paint the ship to keep everything looking 'ship shape and Bristol fashion,' as you say. We do everything that is needed."

Bess looked at Ramjam Buxoo's richly embroidered uniform. There were intricate designs on the scarf around his waist, and he wore a silver chain around his neck that held a small ornament. "What does a serang do?" she asked

"It is my job to make sure that everyone else does his job. That is why I wear the silver pipes. From this they know that I am in charge." He smiled broadly beneath his huge moustache. "The tindal, the kalasis, the bhandary, the paniwallah—they all report to me. I have sailed with the ship from Bombay to Liverpool four times," he said proudly.

Bess didn't really know how to talk to this thin, dark man. She had never met anyone like him. She knew he was a kind of servant, but he was clearly in charge. She could not imagine calling him "boy."

"Do you like sailing?" she asked as politely as possible. She felt it was a stupid question, but she wanted to be polite. Her father had always taught her to be polite.

Ramjam Buxoo laughed. "Yes, little madam. I like to sail. Because of the war, we will get many more rupees. This is good for my family."

They turned a corner and Bess heard loud laughing and cheering. Familiar boys' voices were coming from the cabin ahead.

"Louis!" Bess called, breaking into a run. As she got to the cabin she suddenly remembered her manners and turned to say thank you to Ramjam Buxoo. But he had already vanished, as quietly as he had appeared.

"Bess!" Louis poked his head out of his cabin. "Come see! There's hundreds of sailors on the deck of a ship beside us. It's called the *Duchess of Atholl*." He pulled Bess down the corridor and into a cabin strewn with clothes. "Look! You can see them through Fred's window. I just waved at them and they waved back at me!"

Bess recognized Fred as he jumped up and down by the window. A shy-looking boy with thick glasses was quietly putting his clothes into the dresser. An older boy stood by the door, looking awkward.

"That's Paul," said Fred. The boy with glasses nodded at Bess.

"And that's Rex," said Louis, gesturing to the older boy "Our room's next door, but Fred and Paul've got the best view in here."

Louis and Fred were banging on the round window, trying to get the sailors' attention.

"Don't bang the window so hard!" Bess cried. "You'll break it. Besides, you are making a terrible racket."

Suddenly, they heard a loud pinging sound echoing along the corridor. Louis and Fred rushed to the door. "Michael!" shouted Louis.

Bess looked out and saw Louis's escort jogging down the corridor, bouncing a large ball. Derek and Alan followed him. Louis and Fred fell in, marching and laughing as they headed to the stairs. Rex and Paul joined in and straggled behind.

Bess began to head to the staircase when she was almost knocked over by a small boy as he barrelled down the narrow corridor. "Hey!" she cried as he disappeared around the corner.

"Johnny, wait for us!" a voice behind her called. "Bobby, run ahead and see which direction your brother goes at the next turning."

The boy called Bobby pushed past Bess. His face was as careworn as an adult's, but he couldn't have been much older than Louis. "'Scuse me," he said pulling a lock of thick hair out of his eyes.

"Yes, all right," she said, flattening herself against the wall. "You'd better hurry."

"That Johnny will be the death of me!" said Reverend King to Bess as they passed by. "Ken, can you bring up the rear and make sure that Terry and the others don't get lost?"

Bess watched the reverend lead his troop of boys down the hall. She followed the sounds of laughter and the echo of the bouncing ball up the stairs. Two levels up and she emerged into the open and breathed in the fresh smell of sea air.

She was surrounded by faces that had so quickly become familiar. She saw Ken peering over the railing to look at the water below. Reverend King had little Johnny wriggling under his arm. Louis, Fred, Derek, and Joyce's brother Jack were jumping up trying to get the ball from the ridiculously handsome Michael Rennie. Gussie was trying to keep her brothers and sisters still—a never-ending and seemingly impossible task. Joyce was holding Marion's hand and happily chattering. Rex, who was sharing the cabin with Louis, was standing behind them and Bess could tell just by looking at him that he must be Marion's brother. Eleanor and her roommate Rosemary were leaning on the rail posing glamorously as the wind blew in their faces. Patricia was laughing with Joan, the girl from the cabin next door. And Beth, her absolutely new best friend, was waving her over. Sunshine was glinting off the water and a soft autumn breeze blew her hair.

Bess realized that she was grinning from ear to ear. Her life was beginning. This was the adventure and it was glorious.

Chapter Seven

THURSDAY, SEPTEMBER 12, 1940

The first thing that Sonia saw in her cabin was a huge basket of fresh fruit and chocolate biscuits. *Bon Voyage. Love, Daddy,* said the card. Sonia and Barbara were sharing the cabin, so she supposed she'd have to share the basket. Still, it was more fruit than she'd seen in months.

"I'll have the top bunk," said Barbara as she popped a grape into her mouth. Sonia settled Lolly on the pillow of the lower bunk and carefully hung up her camel-hair coat.

Derek came rushing into their room through the door that connected their cabins. His face was covered in sticky pineapple juice. "Did you see? You can look out the porthole window right into the next boat! It's filled with sailors and they waved at me!"

"Mummy," Barbara called out, "I am going up on deck to write a letter to Alice." Barbara was still angry and sullen about leaving. Sonia knew better than to talk to her when she was in this kind of mood. She decided to change into her new corduroy skirt. She wanted to make a good impression at lunch.

There were beautifully printed menus on their table in the dining room. Sonia's mother told them that they could order anything that they wanted. There was curry and roast chicken and stew and soups—so much food! Derek had to be stopped from ordering one of everything.

There were other passengers sitting in the dining room but very few children. Sonia saw a teenage boy who looked very grown-up and sophisticated travelling with his mother, and she was glad she had changed into her new skirt. Mostly, the huge dining room was filled with adults.

Handsome Captain Nicolls came over to their table to introduce himself. He sat down beside Sonia's mother and began to point out some of the celebrities on the boat.

"That's Lieutenant Colonel James Baldwin-Webb, the MP for Wrekin. He's on his way to New York to try and raise money for ambulances for the Red Cross. Over there, that's Arthur Wimperis, a famous playwright and scriptwriter. Perhaps you saw *The Scarlett Pimpernel*? I understand it did quite well at the box office. Mr. Wimperis is on his way out to Hollywood."

"Who is *that*?" Sonia's mother asked, her eyebrows raised. Sonia couldn't help staring. An exotic-looking woman wearing trousers and a beret was lighting a cigarette.

"That's Ruby Grierson. She's a documentary filmmaker. She is going to be making a movie while we sail," said the captain.

"A movie!" said Derek, wiping brown sauce from the corners of his mouth. "Can I be in it?"

"Well, probably not. It is a movie about the child evacuees. We've got ninety evacuees from the CORB program on board," the captain explained.

"But I'm an evacuee," said Derek. "Aren't I, Mum?"

"Yes, Derek, but these are poor children, travelling without their mummies," their mother explained. "I expect that the movie will be about them because people want to know how the poor are managing during the war. That's right, isn't it, Captain Nicolls?"

"But if they are travelling without their mums, who is looking after them?" asked Barbara. "We don't have to look after them, do we?"

"They have ten volunteer escorts," explained the captain. "Nurses, chaplains, and so forth. Brave bunch of kids. A bit rambunctious. But you won't see much of them. They're at the other end of the ship."

Suddenly, a blond boy about Sonia's age came into the room wearing a bright red puffy silk vest. "Colin," called the captain, "come over and join us."

"What are you wearing that for? Are you a 'vacuee?" demanded Derek, pointing at the vest.

Sonia winced. Derek could be such an embarrassment at times.

"Derek. Manners." said their mother.

"My mother made it for me," said Colin politely. "She couldn't come with me so she made me this special life vest."

"She made it for you?" Sonia was impressed. She couldn't imagine her mother sewing anything.

"Yes," said Colin. "She told me I must never, ever take it off. She said I must even go to bed in it because if we are torpedoed, the vest will keep me afloat until the Royal Navy rescues me."

The captain laughed. "Colin is a passenger, the same as you, Derek," he said. "He is travelling by himself to Montreal."

"When we get to Montreal, I'll get on a train to New York," Colin explained. "There's a family there that are going to look after me while the war's on. The Stickneys. I've never met them but they've already got another couple of English chaps. And they've got two maids. I've promised not to be any trouble."

Sonia watched Colin carefully tuck his napkin over his life jacket. He seemed very calm and self-possessed. She couldn't imagine travelling across the ocean to a foreign country all by herself. She couldn't imagine living with strangers.

"There isn't a chance of our needing to be rescued, is there, Captain Nicolls?" Sonia's mother asked. "I know that some ships have run into U-boats, but with the children on board we're safe, aren't we?"

"Well, there's always a risk, Mrs. Bech, and we take every precaution, of course. But this is a war and the Germans don't always play by the rules." The captain straightened up. "But never you fear. If we had to take to the sea, we'd be well provisioned until we were rescued."

"Excuse me, captain." A small man with a tidy mustache came over to their table.

"Ah, Mr. Davis," the captain said smoothly. "May I introduce you to Mrs. Bech? Mrs. Bech and her three children are sailing with us as far as Montreal."

Mr. Davis took Sonia's mother's hand. "Mrs. Bech. Forgive me for interrupting. The BBC asked me to file a story before we leave port, which I can only do from the captain's bridge. I am so sorry to disturb your lunch."

"Not at all," she said politely.

The captain pushed his chair from the table. "If you will excuse me, I must arrange for Mr. Davis to use the equipment. Then I must see to some final details."

Sonia's mother smiled. "Of course, captain." She turned to Mr. Davis. "I hope perhaps you will join us another time, when you are not so pressed."

Derek stood up and saluted the captain. "Aye, aye sir. When will we set sail?"

Sonia yanked him back down. "You're not a sailor, you know," she hissed at him.

The captain hesitated. "Unfortunately, there's been a bit of a delay to our plans. During all of that bombing last night, the Germans set mines out in the harbour. Our Navy boys have to clear them out of the way before we can get through. Looks like we'll have to wait until tomorrow before we depart."

Tomorrow. Although Sonia was anxious to get going, she knew that one more day wouldn't make that much of a difference now that they were finally on the boat. Their new lives would begin tomorrow.

"That means we'll leave on Friday the thirteenth," said Derek.

"It's always been my lucky day," said Colin. "Are you superstitious?" he asked Sonia.

"Of course not!" said Sonja, suppressing a slight shiver.

Chapter Eight

The ten escorts counted and re-counted their groups, making sure everyone was on deck. Bess knew there were ninety children, but they looked like just a tiny cluster gathered together on the vastness of the ship's deck.

Beyond them, toward the front of the ship, she could see a circle of lascars squatting on the deck. They were eating out of big bowls. A delicious smell of curry wafted over her. Bess couldn't understand a word they were saying, but they seemed to be very happy.

"What a day to be sailing!" Miss Day exclaimed. Ramjam Buxoo was standing beside her smiling. "Now, I don't know about you, but this ship is a lot bigger than I had expected it to be. It would be easy to get lost. So I need you to pay careful attention on our tour.

"You've all been to your cabins. The boys are on the

starboard side of the ship and the girls are on the port side. You must know these terms so that if you do get lost you'll at least know which side of the ship your cabin is on.

"The front of the ship is called the bow. The back of the ship is called the stern. We are standing aft on the main deck. There will be other terms for you to learn as we go along. But right now the most important place that we all need to know how to get to is the dining room. Mr. Buxoo has informed me that they are expecting us."

A great cheer went up.

"Thank you very much," said Ramjam Buxoo, bowing and smiling. "Please to follow me."

Beth linked her arm with Bess. "Did you see that sailor walk by just now? Did you see the way he doffed his hat at us?" asked Beth, breathlessly. "I'd love to know what kind of officer he is."

"Well, we're going to be on the ship for at least a week. I expect we'll learn a lot about sailors and uniforms!" laughed Bess. "Come on, I'm starving!"

Ramjam Buxoo led them inside, to a large open area ringed with a row of expensive looking boutique stores selling jewellery and clothing. There was a sweets shop with tempting jars of dolly mixture, barley sticks, and coconut ice squares. Everyone stopped to peer through the windows.

"It's just like Oxford Street!" said Bess.

"I haven't seen sweets in the stores for almost a year!" said Beth. "I'd love some coconut ice squares."

Louis grabbed Bess's arm. "I want to buy some bull's eyes! Can you give me some of my money?"

A cluster of children peered into the window, excited about buying sweets. Just as they were about to go in, Miss Cornish blocked the doorway.

"Children, we don't have time to be shopping before our meal."

Louis made a face and several of the children started to argue.

Miss Cornish held up her hand for silence. "Also, I need to talk to you about your money. I know that some of you have been given money from home. That money is to help you get started on your new life in *Canada*." Miss Cornish put a special emphasis on the word *Canada*. Bess looked at Louis, but his eyes were glued to the sweets in the shop window.

"Some of the girls in my group have told me that they are worried about carrying their money around. Worried that they might lose it."

Or spend it on sweets, thought Bess.

"We escorts thought it would be a good idea for you to have a bank to keep your money safe, and I have volunteered to be your banker." She held up a small leather purse. "I have a special bag to keep your money in. If you give it to me for safekeeping, I will write down your bank entries, just like a bank teller." She held up a small black ledger book.

"Then, if you need to spend money while you're on the

boat, I'll write down your withdrawals. When we get to Canada, I will give you whatever is left in your account."

"That's a great idea," said Bess loudly. "Louis and I would like to put our money in right now. That way we won't be tempted to spend it," she said, pointedly smiling at Louis. He glared at her as she took a pound note out of her pocket and gave it to Miss Cornish.

"Perfect." She put the note into the bag and opened the book. "I'll write down your deposit, and you sign your name here. That way we both know that I am looking after your money for you."

"Oh, Miss Cornish, can you take mine?" Beth said.

"Miss, here's my tuppence," said a tiny blond boy.

"Miss Cornish, Marion and I have got two shillings!" Rex stepped up, offering his coins.

"I've half-a-nicker," piped in little Joyce.

"Children! Please! I can't look after you all before lunch. Joyce, I'll take your 'half-nicker' now. The rest of you will need to come and find me in the dining room. I am sure there will be lots of time."

Bess noticed that everyone quieted down. No one was fussing about the sweets shop any more. Miss Cornish had a way of speaking that made everyone listen. "Now let's head into dinner. I don't know about you, but I am famished."

At the mention of food, Louis raced down the corridor to the dining room. When Bess caught up to him, he was waiting at the doorway beside a group of lascar stewards dressed in beautiful blue uniforms.

The stewards bowed low and escorted them to a table. The elegant dining room took Bess's breath away. It was set up like a fancy London restaurant, with mounds of fresh fruit on the tables in the middle —bananas, oranges, grapefruits, pineapples —things they hadn't seen since rationing began over a year ago.

Bess, Louis, and Beth sat together. Louis's friend Fred ran up to them chased by a boy with bright mischievous eyes.

"This is Howard," said Fred. "He's in Father O'Sullivan's group. Howard knows almost as much about the Navy as I do."

"Way more!" said Howard.

"We're both gonna be sailors when we grow up," Fred sat down beside Louis. Howard sat on the other side.

An elegant lascar steward came over to their table. "What would the little madams like to eat? Little sirs?"

"Whadda ya mean?" asked Fred. He looked at the others at the table.

Howard opened his eyes wide. "Do you mean I've a *choice* of what to eat?! Isn't there rationing on the ship?"

Bess said the first thing that came into her head. "Ham roll?"

"Roast chicken?" said Beth.

Fred looked around. "Um … bacon buttie?"

"Mince 'n mash?" said Howard.

"Chocolate!" shouted Louis.

"Louis, you have to eat a proper meal," Bess scolded. "Could my brother have a ham roll, please?"

The steward bowed low and went into the kitchen.

'What do you think he'll really bring us?" asked Louis.

"They'll bring us whatever they've planned. Maybe a bit of soup. I am sure they were asking just to be polite. To make us feel special," said Bess. It was all so odd, but then this whole day was like a dream.

"Mebbe they'll bring us a bit a potato? Mebbe there'll be a bit of meat in a stew gravy," said Fred.

"I'd settle for some of that fruit on the table over there," said Beth.

"Can we buy just one jawbreaker at the sweets shop after dinner? Please, Bessie?" said Louis.

"We haven't even left the dock, Louis. Let's wait a bit. The money is safe where it is."

"My auntie gave me four and sixpence before I left. I've never had so much money!" said Howard. "I'm going to go give it to that lady to look after. She looks like my auntie, so I know I can trust her. Auntie! Miss Auntie!" Howard called out in a singsong voice, as he headed across the dining room to Miss Cornish.

"I've got a joey I saved from the Christmas pud," said Fred.

"A joey?" asked Bess. She didn't always understand Fred's accent.

"You know, a thrup'ny bit," said Fred. "That's what we call it in Southhampton. I'm not sure I want to give it over, though. It's my good-luck charm."

"Auntie Mary's got quite a stash!" said Howard as he returned to the table. "She said I can come and see my four and six any time I want."

Just then they were interrupted by the arrival of the steward carrying two fresh, hot rolls filled with thick slabs of York ham. Each was wrapped in a lace cloth and presented on a white china plate. Another steward carried in a soft roll with thick rashers of crispy bacon and a plate of mince and mashed potatoes. A third arrived with a plate of roast chicken, mashed potatoes, carrots, and gravy.

Bess sat there, her jaw dropped. It couldn't be true. No rationing on the boat?

"Is it real?" said Beth.

"Is it magic?" said Fred.

"Who cares?" said Louis, his mouth stuffed with ham roll. "All I know is that this bread is not National Loaf!"

All around them children were ravenously digging into dinners of roast chicken, mince and mash, and steak-and-kidney pie. They asked for seconds, for thirds. And for dessert there was ice cream! Loads of ice cream in any flavour they wanted.

She watched Louis eating. She couldn't remember the last time they had so much food.

People are saying that the war might last for years, she

thought. *Louis will be a young man by the time we get home again. He'll probably be taller than me. Mum and Dad might not even recognize him.* She felt a pang of guilt as she thought of her mother and father. She wished she could send them just a bit of her delicious ham roll.

Another steward arrived and placed a white plate in front of Louis. On it was a box of Cadbury's chocolates.

Chapter Nine

"Hello, boys and girls. My name is Geoffrey Shakespeare, and on behalf of the British government, I would like to welcome all 'seavacuees' to the SS *City of Benares*."

Ken recognized Mr. Shakespeare's name not just because it was the same as the famous playwright's, but also because he had seen his signature on the bottom of the letter from the CORB office that his stepmother had shown him. He was the man who had organized the trip to Canada.

All of the children and escorts were assembled in a huge playroom on the sports deck, one level above the main deck. The playroom was filled with toys and books, and there was the most magnificent rocking horse that Ken had ever seen. It had large baskets on either side, big enough for children to ride in. Gussie was trying to break up a fight between her brothers over who was going to rock and who was going to ride. She was having a hard time keeping them quiet while Mr. Shakespeare talked.

"In this time of war, we want all our children to be safe, and that's why we've arranged to take you across the ocean to people who can look after you until the war is over. We are confident in the convoy, and in the brave men and women who will take you to Canada."

Mr. Shakespeare stood up.

"On behalf of the prime minister of England, I wish you all a bon voyage and look forward to welcoming you back to British soil after this terrible danger has passed. We know that you will be good ambassadors for Britain. You will show the world the British spirit and courage that will win this war!"

Everyone cheered. Terry stretched out his arm to shake hands with Mr. Shakespeare. "On behalf of all of us," Terry said formally, "thank you very much, sir."

"Well put, Terry," said Reverend King.

"And now I turn you over to the ship's chief officer, Officer Hetherington," said Mr. Shakespeare. "Bon voyage!"

"Hello, boys and girls," Officer Hetherington was tall with a serious, grim face and a thick Scottish accent. "I am in charge of the safety of this ship. It is very important that you listen carefully and obey orders at all times. Is that understood?"

Ken nodded seriously. He knew that the chief officer

was just a step down from the captain. He straightened his shoulders.

"There will be lifeboat drills every day while you are on the boat," said Officer Hetherington. He gestured to two cadets. "Cadet Officers Haffner and Critchley are here to give you instructions. It is their job to teach you the rules of the ship and to take you through your lifeboat drills. I leave you in their capable hands."

A cadet officer. That's what I want to be three years from now, thought Ken.

The cadet officers held up heavy-looking blue vests and awkward white, lumpy jackets made of blocks of cork.

"We're going to give each of you a kapok vest and cork life jacket. Your kapok vest must be worn at all times, even when you go to bed," said Cadet Critchley.

Terry elbowed Ken. "How're we gonna sleep in these?" he mouthed silently, as he took the vest.

"These are your life jackets." Cadet Haffner was holding up one of the bulky white jackets. "You don't need to wear them, but you must carry them with you at all times. The good news is that you don't need to carry your gas masks with you. You can leave those in your cabin."

Everyone cheered at the idea of leaving the smelly gas masks behind. Even though Ken was used to carting his everywhere, it was a relief to know that he didn't have to think about gas attacks at sea.

"In the case of an emergency," continued Cadet Haffner,

"you must put your life jackets on immediately. Let's practice by putting them on now."

The cork life jackets were awkward. Ken put his around his neck. Two pieces of cork hung down in front and a large piece was on his back. He pulled the strap tight around his body as Cadet Haffner showed them and felt the hard cork digging into the sides of his chin.

"This feels awful," said one of the girls beside him. "It's bad enough being plump—now I feel like a barrage balloon!"

"Now," Cadet Haffner said, "if you ever need to jump into the water with your life jacket on, there is a very special way to do it."

"Not that any of us *expect* you to have to jump in the water," said Cadet Critchley quickly, "but we have a rule here on the ship that everyone has to know *how* to do it. Even Captain Nicolls had to show us that he could do it before we'd let him run the ship."

Ken knew that wasn't true. Nobody told a captain what to do. But he thought that Cadet Critchley was probably exaggerating for the sake of the younger boys, like Alan and Johnny. He knew they listened better when someone mentioned the captain.

"If you are told to jump off the boat, you must—I repeat *must*—tuck your knees up like this." Cadet Haffner squatted down and grabbed his bent knees, holding them tightly to his chest.

"All right, let's try it. I am going to say 'JUMP!' and when I do, I want to see you all crouch down and grab your knees like I did. All right now? One, two, three, JUMP!"

Ken hugged his knees and watched as all of the others did the same. He saw Derek press his brother Alan down, who immediately started rolling around on the deck like a bowling ball.

"Perfect! All right. Now, if you hear the alarm whistle sound seven times, you must put on your life jacket and walk to your muster station."

"Our what?" asked Alan.

"Your muster station," said Cadet Critchley, "This playroom where we are standing right now is your muster station. If you hear the alarm whistle seven times, just come to the rocking horse.

"Now, let's do a little practice. How many times does a whistle sound for an alarm?"

"Seven!"

"Right. So when you hear seven whistles, what do you go?"

"Go to the mustard station! To the rocking horse!"

"The *muster* station, yes. You walk to the muster station. Do not run. Walk. Then your escort will take you to your lifeboat. So now we are in our muster station, with our life jackets on, and it is time to follow your escort to your lifeboat on the embarkation deck."

"This way, boys," said Reverend King. "We're bound for lifeboat 9." Ken followed his escort up the stairs to the embarkation deck. Their lifeboat was tucked into the open deck high above them.

"How're we supposed to get in that," demanded Johnny, "when it's all the way up there? I can't climb that high."

Reverend King laughed good-heartedly. "Neither can I! Thankfully, we don't have to go up there to the boat; the boat will come down here to us." He bent down to look Johnny right in the face. "Do you understand, Johnny? If you hear the alarm whistle, you and Bobby must go the rocking horse. Then I'll bring you here, to this boat."

He straightened up. "Now let's go over to lifeboat 12. The lascars have lowered that one so that we can see how to get in."

"But I thought this was our lifeboat," said Terry.

"This *is* our lifeboat," explained the reverend patiently. "They are just going to show us how it works with lifeboat 12."

Ken saw all of the other groups heading toward lifeboat 12. "It's just like fire drills at school," he said to Terry as they walked to the port side of the ship. "You have to know how to do them, but you never really need to use 'em."

One of the girls from Miss Hillman's group turned on Ken and Terry. "I was in the *Volendam* when it was torpedoed, and we were sure glad we'd had the drills!"

"You were on the *Volendam*?" said Ken. He'd read all about the ship being hit. He couldn't believe he was actually meeting someone who'd been on it.

"It was exciting, really," she told Ken. "It all happened just like in the drill. Everyone was rescued and we barely even got wet."

Cadet Haffner and the other groups were waiting for them at lifeboat 12. The lifeboat had been pushed forward and was hanging in the air, connected to the ship by heavy ropes. Two lascars were holding handles on a couple of large drums. Ken craned his neck to see. The ropes came out of the drums, went up through large blocks, then through metal levers and down into each end of the lifeboat. "Those are the davids," one of the boys said, proudly pointing at the metal levers.

"Davits," corrected Cadet Haffner, gently. "The ropes you see are called the falls and those drums have reels inside with enough rope on them to lower the boat all the way down to the water."

"Man the falls and reels," commanded Cadet Critchley.

The lascars slowly turned the handles. The ropes got longer, and the lifeboat moved down, stopping in the air beside them.

"You see?" said Cadet Haffner. "The boat comes right down to where you are standing. When you come to your lifeboat, it will already be down, ready for you to step off the deck and get in." He leaned down to one of the little girls. "Now, what is your name?"

"Connie," she said, "Connie Grimmond, mister cadet, sir."

"Connie, would you like to sit in the boat?"

Connie looked scared. "Is it safe? They're not gonna let go, are they?" she eyed the lascars suspiciously. They stood rigidly holding the ropes.

"It's perfectly safe," said Cadet Haffner. "They are trained to hold the boat there until the captain says to lower it. Here, let me go in and show you."

Cadet Haffner nodded to a lascar who took off a section of the guardrail that ran around the edge of the deck. The cadet stepped lightly into the hanging boat and held his hand out to Connie.

"This way, Connie." Ken watched her eye the space between the ship and the lifeboat. Cadet Haffner took hold of her hand. "Just look at the lifeboat, not the space," he said quietly. Connie stepped carefully over the wooden edge. The lifeboat stirred gently.

"That's it. Now sit down on the thwart there," he said guiding her to one of the wooden seats that ran across the boat. "Good girl. That's all there is to it."

Connie beamed up at her brothers and sisters on the deck.

"When everyone is on board the life boat, your officer will say, 'Stand by for lowering.' He'll hold on to this rope, the painter, which will keep the lifeboat attached to the ship until you're ready to cast off," continued Cadet Haffner.

"What are those?" Ken blurted out. He'd been trying to keep quiet during the demonstration, but he had to speak up now. He was the oldest in his group and he didn't want the others to know how excited he was. He pointed to the struts in the centre of the boat. They looked like some kind of complicated gear system.

"Glad you asked that, sailor," said Cadet Critchley. "Those are called the Fleming gears. When you push and pull those levers they turn a propeller shaft below the boat. The propeller then makes the boat move forward. If you are in the lifeboat it will be your job, along with everyone else's, to work the gears and move the lifeboat along. Do you want to try them out?"

Ken's heart leapt. He nodded seriously and stepped carefully into the lifeboat.

"Just grab them on either side, that's right," said Cadet Critchley. "Push forward and then pull backward. Exactly. You're a natural sailor!"

Ken could see himself racing through the water. *When I'm a cadet,* he thought, *I'll be the one showing everyone how to do this.*

"Hey, Ken!" shouted Terry, "I can see the propeller movin'! You're makin' it go!"

Ken beamed. "All right, let's review," said Cadet Critchley. He helped Ken and Connie step out of the lifeboat. The lascars began pulling the ropes to bring it back up to its locked position. Cadet Haffner nodded to the lascar to put the guardrail back.

"When you hear the alarm bell ring seven times, what do you do?" asked Cadet Critchley.

Everyone started yelling at once.

"Put on our life jackets!"

"Walk, don't run, to our muster station!"

"Go to the lifeboat with our escort."

"Get in—when the officer tells us to."

Cadet Critchley raised his hand for everyone to be silent. He knelt down in front of little Joyce. "Now can you tell me, what do you do when you hear that bell?"

Ken watched as Joyce looked into the cadet's eyes. In a quiet and serious voice she said, "I put on my life jacket. I walk, don't run, to the muster station. I go to the lifeboat with Miss Cornish. And I get in when the officer tells me to."

Ken was on the promenade deck, sketching a picture of the *Duchess of Atholl*, the ship berthed beside the *City of Benares*, when the seven whistles sounded for the first alarm drill. He picked up his life jacket and walked calmly to the muster station. As he got there, he heard Bobby frantically explaining to Reverend King that Johnny was lost. Again.

"He always does this. He just goes off exploring. One minute he's beside me and then the next minute he's gone!"

Just then Johnny came running up. "I'm sorry, reverend. It's just that those stairways all look the same. I came as quickly as I could."

Reverend King tried to be patient. "But where is your life jacket, Johnny?"

"Oh, no! I must have left it somewhere. Maybe it's in our cabin. Or maybe I left it in the dining room. I was having a great game of hide and seek with a couple of the boys there. I'll go look!" Johnny started to race off, but the reverend grabbed him and held him back.

"No, you don't. Now that you are here, I want you to stay put. This is just a drill. We'll go through the rest of the drill and then we'll go looking for your jacket."

Ken knew that they had to take the drills seriously. But it was a lovely sunny day and they were sitting safely in the Liverpool harbour. It felt more like going for a picnic than a lifeboat drill. It was hard not to smile.

Three days ago I was still at home with Mollie, he thought. *Three days ago I was still a boy, living at home. Now I am practically a sailor in training, heading to another country across the ocean.*

My life is just beginning.

Chapter Ten

"We're moving! We're finally moving!" Louis came running into Bess's cabin. She'd felt the tremor in the ship when the engines had started, but she hadn't realized they were actually moving.

She leapt off her bunk. She'd been trying to read the book her father had given her, but she kept falling asleep. With all of the air raids, she hadn't had much sleep lately. But she was wide awake now.

"Let's go up on deck," she said. She was shaking with excitement.

They raced down the narrow corridor and up the metal stairs, almost crashing into Miss Hillman who was on her way down.

"Miss Hillman! Did you see? Are we really moving?"

"Yes, Bess, but we are only just leaving the landing stage.

We're heading out to the middle of the river, where we'll anchor until tomorrow morning."

"Tomorrow?! I thought we were leaving today. We're all ready!"

"Apparently, there has been a bit of delay," said Miss Hillman. "But Signalman Mayhew assured me we'll head out sometime tomorrow, probably in the late afternoon."

"I'm going to go find Michael and see if we can have a football game," said Louis, pouting.

Bess sighed. "This waiting is awful."

"Why don't you head up to the playroom and find Beth?" said Miss Hillman. "I think I saw her heading up there. There are shelves of great books. I'm sure you'll find something you'll like."

Bess wondered if Miss Hillman had read her mind. The last thing she wanted to do was to go back to her cabin and try to read *Freedom and Democracy*.

But when she got to the playroom, it was pandemonium. The five- and six-year-olds were playing a loud game of tag, running and screaming everywhere. Eleanor was turning a jump rope with Patricia. Joyce and Marion were skipping and laughing. Beth was braiding Joan's hair.

"I'm so glad you've come up," said Beth to Bess. "Isn't this waiting horrid?!"

"I know," said Bess. "I really thought we were on our way. But Miss Hillman says it won't be until tomorrow."

There was a group of children writing letters at a table in

the corner of the room. Ken, the boy with the large overcoat was there, hunched over. Bess could see that he was writing an illustrated letter—there were drawings of different parts of the *Benares* and many lines of writing.

"It's our last chance, if we want to send something home," said Beth. "Cadet Critchley said they'll take letters to shore and mail them before we head out."

"Oh, that's all right," said Bess. "I'm going to wait. I'll write a long one as we sail. That way I can send it with a Canadian stamp once we've landed."

"Maybe we could give Gussie a hand," suggested Beth. Gussie was sitting with her sisters and brothers. She was obviously trying to write her own letter, but her little brothers didn't know how to write yet, so she was trying to teach them, and keep them from fighting.

"Here, Gussie," said Beth, "shall we write out the letters for your brothers so you can write your own?"

Gussie looked up at Bess and Beth with grateful eyes. "That'd be nice. I've got ever so much I want to say to our mum, but I also want her to hear from Eddie and Lenny. Connie 'n Violet, they're all right. They know how to write."

"I'm tellin' 'em about the playroom, an' the rockin' horse," said Violet.

"An' I'm tellin' 'em about getting in the lifeboat!" said Connie proudly.

Bess sat down beside little Lenny. "What would you like

me to write?" she asked, gently pulling the paper in front of her.

"I want to tell mum 'bout the gulls. We gave 'em a bit of our biscuit an' they started peckin' and fightin' and screamin'!" said Lenny excitedly.

"Can you write about the lifeboats?" Eddie asked Beth. "Can you tell our mum about how we practice to jump into the sea?"

Bess and Beth wrote out Lenny and Eddie's letters while Gussie wrote to her parents and to her older sister Kathleen. "You'd like our Kathleen," she said to Bess. "She's smart like you. She's too old to come with us now, but she's goin' to come to live with me in Canada, when the war's over. Maybe you'll visit us when she comes."

When the war is over. Children grow so quickly, thought Bess. She looked at little Lenny. *Would he even remember his sister Kathleen?*

* * *

Ken sat on a deck chair. He'd finished his letter to Mollie and was trying to draw the *Duchess of Atholl*. This was his third try. The ship was so close that he couldn't take it all in. He settled on sketching some of the details that he could see—the bridge, a lifeboat. Then he looked back to the pier and began drawing one of the cargo ships.

"Not bad."

The voice made him jump. He'd been so focused on the drawing that he'd forgotten completely where he was. He looked up to see a young sailor, not much taller than him, squinting in the sunshine.

"This one, the *Marina*, that's my favourite. Built in '35. Mate of mine's on her crew."

"How long have you been in the Royal Navy?" Ken asked.

"'Enlisted in '39. Right at the start. Way to see the world, you know. An' I've always been good at codes."

"Codes?"

"Codes, cyphers, puzzles. That's why they trained me up as a signalman. Signalman Mayhew," he said, saluting. He took out a packet of cigarettes. "Guess I can't offer you one of these!" he laughed. "How old are you?"

"I'm thirteen, sir," Ken felt embarrassed by his short pants, his thin arms and legs.

"Ah, well, you'll be joinin' up in no time. I've just turned nineteen myself. The next six years'll be your best," he winked.

Ken wondered where he'd be in six years. *Right here*, he thought, *on the deck of a ship, in uniform.*

"Yup," the signalman continued, "the only problem is the waitin'. When you're ready to go, you're ready. But we've got to wait for the commodore and the rest of them to show up."

"The commodore? Aren't we under the command of Captain Nicolls?" Ken was thirsty for information about the workings of the ship.

"Commodore Mackinnnon's in charge of the convoy."

"The convoy?!" said Ken. His voice had squeaked with excitement and he hoped that Signalman Mayhew hadn't noticed.

"Yup. Safety in numbers. If a U-boat tries to torpedo a ship in a convoy, the other ships'll attack it and rescue the boat that's hit."

Ken had read about convoys. He knew that they had to have a lead ship.

"Who's the lead?" he asked, trying to sound as knowledgeable as possible.

"HMS *Winchelsea*."

The *Winchelsea*! Ken knew all about the *Winchelsea*. He'd read about her battles in the Great War. He couldn't believe she was going to be sailing with them. He couldn't wait to draw her.

"And we'll have a couple a corvettes aside us," Mayhew continued. "They're like tiny destroyers. Can do a lot of damage to a U-boat, they can. And at the start we'll have a Sunderland flying boat with submarine-killer depth charges that can blow a U-boat clear outta the water, watchin' us from the air."

Ken had drawn hundreds of Sunderlands in the Wembley library. He realized that he was sitting with his mouth wide open. He coughed and tried to rearrange his face so that he didn't look like such a stupid little kid.

"Yup," Mayhew went on, "we're goin' in convoy with

eighteen other ships. Eighteen! We'll stretch three miles over the ocean! You're going to Canada in style, mate."

That night, Ken lay in his bunk in the dark thinking about what a great day it had been. He'd had lots to eat, had explored the whole ship. He'd written his letter to Mollie. He began to drift off to sleep, with a happy grin on his face.

BANG! Suddenly, there was an ear-splitting crash and the boat rocked. He was awake instantly. Another bang. The boat rocked even more.

"What is it?" Terry called from the bunk below. "What's happenin', Ken?" His voice sounded small in the dark.

"I think it's a raid. A raid on the docks," said Ken. He tried to make his voice sound calm. He counted the seconds between each hit and tried to imagine how close they were to the ship. The ship rocked with every crash.

"Are we gonna get bombed? Where's the shelter?"

"No shelter on the ship, Terry. But it's okay. They don't really aim for the ships. They're aimin' for the docks." Ken tried to make his voice sound more confident than he actually felt.

The cabin door opened. "What's happening?"

Derek and his brother Alan were holding hands in the doorway. Ken could just barely see them. The ship was blacked out and there was virtually no light. They had to have blackout conditions on the water. A single light, even just from a torch, would make them an easy target for the bombers.

It was one thing to be in an air-raid shelter during a bombing raid. It was quite another to be sitting out in the open, in a huge boat, rocking from side to side. The bombs seemed so close.

Ken heard Alan sniffle. "Derek, I want Mum." His voice was strained.

Just then the tall figure of Reverend King filled the doorway. "What are you boys doing up?" he asked.

"Alan's a little scared, reverend," said Derek. His voice was shaky.

"Nothing to be scared of. It's just Jerry's way of saying goodbye to us. Nothing to worry about at all." The reverend's voice sounded strained, like he was working hard at sounding cheerful.

There was another crash, and the boat rocked fiercely. "Just think about the great football game you're going have on the deck tomorrow morning with Mr. Rennie," said the reverend, as he steadied himself on the doorframe.

Alan was sniffling even louder.

"Here, Alan," said the reverend, reaching into the pocket of his dressing gown. "Here's a cookie that I saved from dinner. I'm sure that will make you feel better. Sorry I don't have any more for the rest of you boys."

"That's all right, reverend," said Terry, but his voice

sounded thick with fear.

Another crash. The boat rocked.

"Need to get you boys back to your own room," said the reverend.

Derek started to cry. "I don't know how to look after Alan. I don't know what to do," his voice started to get louder as the tears started to flow.

The reverend knelt down. "That's all right, Derek. You aren't alone. You know that, don't you? Look, I've got something special for you. It's my good-luck charm. It'll bring both you and Alan good luck."

Through the darkness, Ken could just see the reverend handing something to Derek. It was small and white and fit into the palm of his hand.

"What is it?" Derek asked.

"It's a lamb. Not a real one of course. It's a special charm made from Bakelite," he laughed. "Think of it as the lamb of God. It will protect you. All of you," Reverend King said, straightening up. "Now, time to head off to your own beds, boys, so that Terry and Ken can get some sleep."

Sleep. How could he sleep as the ship rocked with each crash? He needed to stop thinking about the bombers, to try and stop imagining the massive airplanes dropping their bombs so close by. Ken squeezed his pencil and notebook tightly every time he heard a crash. He tried hard to think about sailing tomorrow. He remembered sitting in the lifeboat, pushing and pulling on the Fleming gears, the boat gently swaying beneath him. He imagined that the crashes were the sound of the sailors applauding him for his great work with the levers. Cadet Sparks. He let the ship rock him to sleep as though he was a baby.

Chapter Eleven

When morning came, it brought with it a thick fog and mist. *The fact that it was overcast last night probably saved us*, thought Ken. The Germans probably didn't see the dark, camouflaged ship at anchor in the middle of the river.

After breakfast, Ken sat on his bunk drawing, interrupted only by the routine of four lifeboat drills. *Just filling time*, thought Ken impatiently.

But just before lunch, Terry came running in.

"The commodore's come on board! And the *Duchess of Atholl*'s left! That means the harbour's cleared of mines!" he shouted. "We'll be leavin' soon!"

It was Commodore Mackinnnon's job to guide all eighteen of the ships in convoy. And now the commodore was on the same ship as Ken.

He wondered how hard it would be to sneak a look into the bridge. Maybe tomorrow, after the rest of the convoy had joined them.

It was six o'clock in the evening on Friday, September 13, 1940, when the SS *City of Benares* left its mooring buoy and sailed down the River Mersey, out of the estuary and into the bay. Bess, Ken, and all of the seavacuees stood midship on the main deck waving Union Jacks and singing, "Wish me luck as you wave me goodbye!"

Inside the luxurious passengers' lounge at the stern of the ship, Sonia peered through the porthole windows. A golden sunset lit up the harbour. She could see sailors on the other ships smiling, waving and cheering as the *City of Benares* glided past. Behind her, the adult passengers in the lounge raised glasses of champagne in a toast. "To England!"

They were on their way.

PART II

Chapter Twelve

When Bess woke up on Saturday morning, there was no sign of land. She looked through the porthole window and saw other ships sailing in formation beside the *Benares*. The convoy must have joined them during the night.

The sky and the water were the same shade of grey. The ship was rolling around on the waves. The movement reminded Bess of a fun ride at the fair. She headed up to the dining room for breakfast with Beth, laughing and bouncing off the corridor walls as the ship pitched.

But by the time the stewards brought them their eggs and rashers of bacon, Bess was weak and sweaty. Her stomach was churning. She took one look at breakfast and rushed outside, making it to the rail just in time to throw up over the side. Beth joined her a minute later.

"This is horrible," moaned Beth, wiping her mouth.

"Friends who vomit together, stay together?" said Bess. She took her glasses off and leaned over the water, hoping the cool wet spray would make her feel better.

"I've got to get back to my cabin. I've got to lie down," said Beth, clutching the rail.

"Me too," said Bess weakly.

As they rounded the corner near their cabins, Bess saw Annie Ryan, one of the navy stewardesses, helping Eleanor down the corridor.

"Oh, dear, another two casualties. Get yourselves into bed and I'll be right in with something to ease your tummies," she said cheerfully.

"Thank you, Miss Ryan." Bess mumbled.

"It's Annie, Just plain Annie. Now, don't you worry. We'll have you right as rain soon enough."

As Bess crawled into her bed she heard a terrible retching noise in the bathroom and realized that her cabin mate, Patricia, was also sick.

Annie came in with mugs of barley water. "Try and drink a bit of this," she said, handing them each a mug. Bess couldn't imagine swallowing anything, but Annie insisted that a bit of the barley water would calm her stomach.

"When is it going to stop?" Patricia moaned. "I hate this. This never happened on the *Volendam*. I wish I were home," she whispered softly.

"There, there," said Annie. "This is just a bit of seasickness.

We're in a storm, that's all. The steward says that we've got some bad weather to get through, but then we'll be sailing into the sunshine."

Bess's head was spinning. She wasn't sure she could make it from her bunk to the toilet and was terrified that she'd throw up on her bed.

"Oh, dear, Bess, you do look a bit green. I'll go fetch you a bucket."

Bess felt sweat dripping into her hair. At the same time, she felt cold and began to shiver. She was aware of Annie sponging her face with a soft warm flannel. She tried to still her breathing.

"Just relax. That's it. See if you can sleep." Annie's voice drifted into her ears. Perhaps the barley water had helped. Perhaps a little nap ...

* * *

Ken woke up feeling terrifically hungry. He got up and dressed. Why couldn't he have any long trousers? It was ridiculous. Short trousers didn't make any sense on a ship. He put on his overcoat, and shoved his notebook and pencil into the pocket. Terry was softly moaning in bed, so Ken left him and headed to the dining room.

Miss Day greeted him at the entrance. There were hardly any children in the dining room. "My, you've got a good strong stomach, haven't you?" she said. "Here, you three should eat together. Louis and Fred, make some room for Ken. Aren't many going to come in for their breakfasts. You'll get as much as you can eat this morning, that's for sure."

Louis looked up at him with a full mouth of fried potatoes. "We've got the place to ourselves," he said. "My sister Bess was here for a minute, but then she went outside to throw up. A lot of them have been throwing up over the rails."

"There's lots didn't even get outta bed," said Fred. "But I feel great!"

"Me too," said Ken, as he helped himself to a huge steaming plate of scrambled eggs, with thick rashers of bacon. "Here's to life on the high seas!"

He had several portions of eggs, bacon, potatoes, and toast, congratulating himself on his strong stomach.

"Let's go out on deck! I want to feel the sea spray in my face," said Louis. Ken thought it sounded like a line he'd read in a book, but he also thought it would be a great feeling to stand outside as the ship cut through the waves.

"Bet I can spit farther than you can," said Fred, knocking over his chair as he raced to the door.

The wind hit them as soon as they walked out on deck. Ken hadn't realized how loud the sea would be. The ship smashed through the waves, rising and falling through crest and trough. Their boat had seemed enormous when they were in the harbour. Now, with nothing but ocean on the horizon, it felt like a tiny speck.

The sea spray smacked their faces. It wasn't cold, but it sure was wet. As soon as they got to the rail, Fred spit out into the wind. But the spit flew backward toward them!

"Look out!" Ken laughed.

"Let me try!" said Louis, puckering up his mouth.

"Hey, you lot," a voice growled behind them. Ken turned to see Gunner Peard glowering. He'd seen Peard before, sitting lookout in his gunner's nest. He was short, incredibly muscular, and gruff. He looked like he could take on most of the German army all by himself. He was the oldest sailor he'd seen on the boat and Ken was afraid they were in trouble.

"You've got to put some muscle into those lips to get a good spit out. Like this." Peard horked a mighty gob of spit and managed to hit a passing sea gull. The three of them exploded with laughter.

"Come on then. I'll show you my lookout."

Peard strode toward the bow. The boys had to race to keep up with him. "Now I can't take you up on my crow's nest—leastways, not until you've had a bit more experience as a sailor," he said. "But you can watch how I climb up there."

Quick as a flash, he was climbing up the rope ladder high, high above their heads. "How 'bout I spit from up here?" he yelled down at them. Ken covered his head. Peard laughed and slid back down the rope, barely touching the rungs.

"Do you watch out for submarines from up there?" Fred asked.

"No, they'd be a bit hard to see from up there. It's my job is to watch for Focke-Wulf Condors," Peard said proudly. "Those are Jerry's special aircraft that are out looking for us. If they spot us, they tell their submarine buddies where to find us."

"And what would happen if you saw one of them?" Louis asked, wide-eyed.

"Well, I'd get on one of those six-inch anti-aircraft guns on the bow and blow them out of the sky," said the gunner proudly.

"Will you let us know if you see one? Please?" Fred was jumping up and down with excitement.

Ken looked at Gunner Peard. Then he looked across the rolling sea at all of the ships in convoy, just the way that Signalman Mayhew had said they'd be. He'd be happy for it to be like this forever. He didn't care if they ever got to Canada.

* * *

Sonia was drinking little sips of tea. They'd had a tray brought to the room, with a silver tea service. There were soft-boiled eggs in little eggcups, and thin toast soldiers to dip. Barbara was really sick. A nurse had been in to see her earlier. Derek and their mother were sleeping in the next room. Sonia's stomach was a bit rocky, but she'd had a bit of egg and really felt fine. She was sitting in bed pretending that she was a princess, escaping from the war. She imagined coming back from Canada, with crowds lining the streets and cheering. She'd be older, of course, and a prince, maybe a Scottish one, would see her looking pale but brave as she waved from the open car to the people, her people. She took another sip from the thin china cup.

A knock on the door startled her from her daydream. Barbara moaned softly. Sonia crept quietly to the door and opened it a crack. Colin was standing there in his bright red life jacket, grinning from ear to ear.

"Oh good, you're up! Everyone else is down for the count. Want to go to the lounge and see if we can find the captain? I'd love to know our position."

"Be with you in a tick," said Sonia. She got dressed as quietly as she could, making sure to put her kapok vest over her cardigan. She grabbed her life jacket and headed out into the hall. She loved this feeling of freedom, of being special while everyone else was sick.

"Mother says our family have always been good sailors, but I'm the only one up today," she said to Colin. "I guess that's because I take after Father."

"Never felt better, myself," said Colin.

A sudden lurch of the ship sent them both skidding into the wall of the corridor. Colin laughed. "You can sure tell we're at sea! Nothing like it back home!"

They slid from side to side as they worked their way down the corridors and into the lounge. A few of the adult passengers were there reading, playing cards, and drinking tea. Mr. Davis, the man from the BBC, looked up when they walked in and gave them a wave before scowling down at his papers.

"Maybe he's writing about us for the radio," Sonia said to Colin.

"Look at all of these empty chairs," said Colin. "Come on over here. We can build a great hiding place. No one will find us!"

Sonia helped Colin haul together eight chairs to build a fort in the corner of the lounge. They stacked them up so that they were completely hidden from view.

"Here, this will make it perfect," said Colin. He grabbed one of the white tablecloths from off a table and draped it over the upturned chairs.

"It's kind of like a teepee," he said, smiling at his handiwork.

"And no one is using these," said Sonia, picking up a deck of cards from a side table. "Do you know how to play Happy Families?"

They settled themselves under the chairs, Sonia using her life jacket as a cushion. But suddenly the ship pitched and the chairs slid and started to fall on top of them.

"Look out!" Sonia yelled. Colin grabbed at the falling chair.

"Quiet over there, you two," said a gruff adult voice from the other side of the lounge.

"Sorry, sir," Colin called out. "Here," he said to Sonia quietly, "this'll be a bit steadier." He laid the chairs down, making a circle. "More like a wagon train than a fort, but I don't suppose anyone really minds."

He put two chairs in the centre of the circle and draped the cloth over them. There was just enough room for them to fit under unnoticed.

Colin was dealing out the cards when a man's voice spoke quite close to them. "Allow me, Miss Grierson." Sonia heard the sound of a cigarette lighter.

"Thank you, Mr. Nagorski. So kind." Ruby Grierson's gravelly voice preceded the distinct smell of cigarette smoke.

"They don't know we're here," mouthed Sonia to Colin.

"You are untroubled by the stormy seas, Miss Grierson?"

"No, I'm not bothered at all. However, many of the children are down. No point in trying to do much filming today." Sonia heard the woman take a drag on her cigarette.

"A shame," said Mr. Nagorski. "Seasickness is a terrible affliction. I am thankful not to suffer from it." He spoke with a soft, formal voice. While his English was very good, Sonia could tell that he was a foreigner.

"I had it the first few times I crossed. I can just imagine how miserable those little kids are. I saw a couple of them throwing up over the side this morning. Not something I really wanted to film." Miss Grierson laughed softly.

"But I did get a good photograph out on deck this morning," she continued. "A nice shot of some boys with one of the sailors. They weren't sick. They were learning how to spit into the wind, I think."

Sonia and Colin had to stuff their hands in their mouths so as not to laugh and give themselves away.

"Ah, yes, young boys. The same in every country in the world."

Sonia could easily imagine Derek in a spitting contest. Mother would have a fit.

"I am fascinated by your project, Miss Grierson," Mr. Nagorski continued. "Why is it that your British Broadcasting Corporation is interested in these children? Why have they hired you to make this movie?"

Smoke wafted down to where Sonia and Colin were eavesdropping. Sonia held her nose so that she wouldn't sneeze.

"Well, Mr. Nagorski, these kids are a kind of experiment. The English government has launched one of the greatest sociological experiments of all time."

Sonia still couldn't figure out why *those* children were so special. They were all of them leaving England. Colin was travelling without his parents, just like the children at the other end of the boat. Why was Miss Grierson's movie only about the children at the other end of the boat, the ones who couldn't pay for the trip?

"Never before have so many children been evacuated—sent to the countryside, shipped to other countries—leaving parents and family behind. Never before has a country paid millions of pounds to send a generation away. A hundred thousand children sent to Wales alone! And now this CORB plan to send another hundred thousand across the ocean to the colonies: New Zealand, Australia, South Africa, Canada—and many more to America. They estimate that more than a million children are going to be sent away over the next few months.

"They say that since all of the children have gone, London is now a city without heart. Perhaps England will become a whole country without a heart, without a future."

"There are many without a future now," said Mr. Nagorski quietly. "My city, my country, is now lost to me. I am one of the lucky ones. I escaped before the invasion. I will have a future, a future in America where my wife and daughters already await me. But for many thousands in Poland, there is no future. There is only death."

Miss Grierson spoke gently. "This is what the English fear; that England will fall as Poland has. We were not there for Poland. We did not help. And if England is invaded, we fear there will be no help for us.

"And so we send our children away while we can. We English hope, we believe, that our children will return one day. But no one knows how long will they be gone or what they will be like when they come back. Will there be an England? Will there be parents for them to come back to? How will it be for parents to meet grown-up children, with different accents and different ideas?"

Sonia hadn't thought of the evacuation this way. For her, it felt more like a long holiday than anything else. Might she be so changed that her own father wouldn't know her when she got back? Would she end up with one of those horrid American accents? And for the children at the other end of the boat, might they never know any of their family again?

"Ah, but I've disturbed you, Mr. Nagorski," said Miss Grierson. "I can see you want to get back to your book."

"Not at all, Miss Grierson. I am grateful for your conversation. It has been a long time since I have felt safe to talk of such things," he replied.

"I fear I am not yet able to conceive of a time of peace," he continued sadly, "but for the moment I can feel a kind of contentment. Even with this storm of nature, life on board our SS *City of Benares* seems full of ease and refinement. It is a life we must allow ourselves to enjoy. For whatever time we are allowed."

Chapter Thirteen

SUNDAY, SEPTEMBER 15, 1940

"Eggs have never tasted this good!" said Bess, helping herself to a second portion.

They had passed through the storm at some point in the middle of the night. Sunday morning dawned calm and sunny. Everyone came to the dining room cheerfully, as though the awful seasickness had never happened. There were steaming mugs of sweet tea, hot fresh rolls with butter, and double helpings of eggs and bacon. Bess was starving.

"Hey, Louis!" Fred and Howard rushed up to the table. Howard grabbed a couple of rashers of bacon and shoved them into a roll.

"Fred and I are goin' to the other end of the ship to see the toffs. Wanna come?"

Louis leapt up. Bess glared at him.

"Finish your meal first," she said sternly.

"You're not Mum," Louis grumbled.

"No, but you know that Mum would want you to finish your breakfast."

"How come Fred and Howard can go?"

"Because Fred and Howard don't have an older sister to look after them."

"I didn't ask you to look after me!"

"No, but Mum did."

"See you after breakfast, Lou," said Fred as he and Howard raced out of the dining room.

Louis looked down at his plate of eggs and bacon. "Do you think Mum misses us?" He pushed the eggs around with his fork.

"Oh, Louis, of course she does. She was really sad when we left, but she knows it's for the best." Bess couldn't help feeling a twinge of guilt at how much pressure she'd put on her mother to let them both go. She hadn't really thought about what it might mean to Louis.

By the time they'd finished breakfast it was too late for Louis to go down to the other end of the ship. It was time to go up to the sports deck, where Reverend King was going to lead a Sunday morning service. Father O'Sullivan, the boys' other escort, was supposed to do it, but the priest had come down with a terrible flu and was confined to bed.

Fred and Howard caught up with them as they left the dining room.

"You should've seen 'em, Lou. There's a boy, 'bout my age, wearin' a funny bright red jacket," said Howard.

"And a girl that Howard said was pretty!" teased Fred.

"Did not!" glared Howard.

Bess smiled over at Beth as they took their seats. The reverend began the hymn with his rich baritone voice. Everyone joined in.

> Each little flower that opens,
> each little bird that sings,
> God made their glowing colours,
> and made their tiny wings.

It felt wonderful to sing outside in the sunshine. The water sparkled. How extraordinary it was not to see any land, anywhere. Nothing but water and the convoy of ships.

> All things bright and beautiful,
> all creatures great and small,
> all things wise and wonderful:
> the Lord God made them all.

Bess looked around her at all of the children. She looked out over the vastness of the ocean. *We are so small*, she thought.

> The purple-headed mountains,

the river running by,
the sunset and the morning
that brightens up the sky.

She looked at the ships in convoy: Nine rows, two ships deep. Eighteen ships to get them to Canada. Three miles wide. She felt so proud.

All things bright and beautiful,
all creatures great and small,
all things wise and wonderful:
the Lord God made them all.

"We send our prayers to our fathers, mothers, and loved ones back in England. We pray for their safety and bravery," offered Reverend King. "We also pray for Father O'Sullivan, and wish him a speedy recovery from his flu.

"Heavenly Father, hear our prayers for Captain Nicoll and Commodore MacKinnon that they may guide us safely through these waters. And we pray for Prime Minister Churchill, as he wages war against our terrible enemies."

Bess was sure that England would win the war. She and all of the other children were all leaving so that no one had to look after them. They were leaving so that the war would be easier to win. Seasickness and homesickness were small prices to pay.

The service ended and Miss Day stood up to address them.

"I am glad to see everyone looking better today," she said, beaming. "We've got a couple of activities planned, so please listen carefully.

"First of all, there will be lifeboat drills today. You know what that means. We expect you to remember the rules: Wear your kapok vest. Carry your life jacket with you at all times. When you hear the alarm, walk to your muster station and await instructions.

"Also, Miss Gilliat-Smith is offering a drawing class in the playroom after dinner today. There will be a competition and all of the drawings that are submitted will have a special showing in the first-class passenger lounge. The winner will receive a box of chocolates, donated by Captain Nicoll!"

At this a great cheer went up. Bess saw Ken take out his journal. It seemed whenever she saw him he was drawing. So different from Louis, she thought. Louis had a hard time sitting for two minutes at a time.

"Speaking of the passengers," Miss Day continued, "a number of you have been looking through the fence at the stern end of the deck and watching the first-class passengers. Please remember that it is rude to stare. There are some very important people on this ship and they do not want to be looked at like zoo animals. Remember your manners and stay to our end of the ship."

Bess wondered if this message was aimed at Fred and

Howard. She saw them exchange sly glances.

"However, there is one passenger from the other end of the ship who very much wants you to talk to her. I would like to introduce Miss Ruby Grierson."

"Wow," said Beth, her eyes wide.

"Holy moly," said Howard.

Bess thought she had never seen anyone so glamorous. Miss Grierson was tiny and slim. She wore a beret, like a Frenchman, and she was wearing trousers like a man!

"Hello, boys and girls. My name is Ruby Grierson, but I'd like you to call me Ruby."

Ruby spoke in a low gravelly voice. She gestured with a long cigarette holder, inhaling elegantly.

"I have been asked to make a movie about this special trip across the sea, a movie about *you*."

"A movie?" Louis nudged Bess. "Did she say we're going to be in a movie?"

"I'm gonna to be in pictures! My mum can see me at the picture show!" squealed Fred excitedly.

Ruby was smiling. "I am afraid I am going to be quite a pest. I'll be asking you all kinds of questions and filming you throughout the voyage. As a special thank you, I'm organizing a tea party in the dining room tomorrow. We'll have decorations and games and lots of scones and jam and butter, fairy cakes, and ice cream."

Beth looked at Bess. "Cake *and* ice cream?"

"I think it will be great fun. I only have one rule."

Ruby pointed at them with her cigarette holder. Everyone was quiet.

We'd all agree to any rule, thought Bess, *for fairy cake and ice cream.*

"You can watch what I am doing, and you can ask me any questions. But if I am in the middle of filming, do not interrupt. Understand? Is that a deal?" Everyone was nodding, dazed. Ruby Grierson was mesmerizing. She was speaking words that they hadn't heard since rationing: *Tea party. Scones and jam and butter. Cakes and ice cream.*

"So, I'll see you at the party, shall I?"

There was thunderous applause and cheers from everyone.

Miss Day gestured for quiet. "Well, that is something to look forward to, isn't it? For now, you have some free time to write letters or read your books. Make sure you tell your escort where you are going to be. Escorts, please gather up the little ones, the five- and six-year-olds, and bring them to the playroom. We are setting up a nursery area with the help of some of the older girls."

Miss Day had already asked Bess and Beth if they would help out with the nursery. Joyce automatically slipped her hand into Bess's, while Beth went off to try and round up Eddie Grimmond.

Playing with little children, taking a drawing class, going to a tea party, meeting an exotic filmmaker ... the war seemed very far away.

Chapter Fourteen

Bess and Beth had a group of the little girls out on the sports deck playing jump rope. Nearby, Michael Rennie was playing tug-of-war with the boys, on top of the boarded-up swimming pool. Bess had one eye on the girls, but she couldn't help watching the game.

"Pull! Harder ... harder ..." Louis' team was struggling and straining. Suddenly they fell over and the rope flew from their hands.

"Too bad," said Michael, "but that means your team gets to be first up for the next game. Time to practise for the Wild West!"

He took the rope and knotted it into a loop.

"He's good at everything, isn't he?" Beth had stopped turning the rope for the girls.

"Mmm ..." agreed Bess.

"The boys worship him," said Beth.

"Louis told me that he's built his own racing cars," said Bess. She watched Michael swing the rope above his head, flick it out and neatly lasso a deck chair. All the boys cheered and clapped.

"Can I try? Show me next! Please, Michael?" The boys were jumping up and down all around him. Michael handed the thick rope to Louis. Louis tried to swing it over his head, but it was so heavy he could barely lift it off the deck.

"And I heard he was a star rugby player at Oxford," said Beth. "He's just on this trip for a bit of a lark before going back to school."

Bess wondered if it would be very unladylike to swing a lasso. She imagined Ruby Grierson could pull it off ...

"We still playing jump rope, then?" Violet tugged on Bess's arm, interrupting her thoughts.

The tea party was everything they hoped it would be. The dining room was decorated with coloured streamers and balloons. Every table was piled high with scones. There were bowls of thick cream and strawberry jam. The stewards carried in slices of fairy cake with scoops of ice cream.

The room was filled with the sounds of laughter, noisemakers, and snapping party crackers. Bess and Beth sat at a table with Joyce, Marion and her brother Rex, and Gussie with her sisters and brothers. Bess helped Joyce put a party hat on her teddy bear Winchell, and showed her how to blow the horn to make a noise.

Louis ran over to their table. "Look what I got in my party cracker! A compass!"

"Now you'll always know what direction we are travelling," she said, as he rushed back to his table with Fred and Howard.

"Boys and girls!" Miss Day called for attention. "I know you are all having a wonderful time and that you'd like to say a special thank you to Miss Grierson."

The room exploded in cheers and whoops. Ruby Grierson acknowledged them all with a wave of her cigarette holder.

"Also," Miss Day continued, "I have very good news for you. Captain Nicolls has just informed me that that our Royal Air Force shot down a record 185 German planes yesterday!"

Everyone cheered and applauded long and hard.

"Sounds like the war is almost over!" said Beth to Bess. "Surely the Germans can't last much longer. Maybe we'll get to Canada and turn right back!"

"But we are not out of the woods yet," Miss Day reminded them. "You must always remember to have your life jackets with you at all times. And even though it is awkward, you must continue to sleep in your clothes and kapok vests. Now, back to your cake."

Bess watched Gussie trying to wipe ice cream from Eddie's

nose while Lenny swooped around the table pretending to be an airplane.

"*Rat-a-tat-a-tat!*" Lenny screeched.

She carefully poured some milky tea for Connie and Violet. Suddenly, Lenny knocked her arm and the tea went flying.

"Hey, stupid! Now look what you've done!" Ken jumped up. He'd been sitting at a quiet table behind the Grimmonds, working on his drawing for the contest. Now it was covered in tea, ruined.

"I'm sure he didn't mean it. It was just an accident," Bess said. She took her napkin and tried to dab at the drawing.

"It was no good anyway," Bess heard Ken mumble as he stormed away from the party.

* * *

Ken knew he shouldn't have gotten angry. He shouldn't have called that boy stupid. But he was tired of being around little kids all of the time. Terry was always following him, asking him what he was drawing, what he was writing. And since the day of the storm he'd also had Louis and Fred, and now Howard, on his heels. They just wanted to play all day. He was older. He didn't want the sailors seeing him with those little kids. The tea party was nice, but it didn't matter to him. What mattered was the ship.

He strode along the deck, trying to look taller in his

oversized overcoat. He stood at the rail and looked across the water to the freighters and corvettes sailing in convoy. He craned his neck to see the HMS *Winchelsea* at their head. It was so huge, so imposing. His drawing hadn't shown that at all. He'd try again, but this time he'd draw one of the corvettes beside it, to show the scale.

He needed to find a good place to sketch. A place where no one would come bothering him. He looked up at the sports deck. Terry would find him there for sure. The next level up was the embarkation deck. Not much up there other than the bridge and the lifeboats. He knew he'd be in trouble if he went in sight of the bridge—Reverend King had explained that they had to stay behind the bridge so as not to get in the way of the captain.

He looked up at the lifeboats. They were secured, slung in on their davits. He thought they were probably high enough that he could see over the bow of the ship. They were covered with tarps, but he was sure he could probably loosen one enough to get inside. No one would find him there. Could he climb up the davit and get in? Did he dare?

* * *

Sonia was in the passenger lounge, covered in sticky cherry juice. She'd dabbed a bit of it on her cheeks to make them look rosy, the way her mum did with her makeup. She'd tried to trace some on her lips like lipstick. Mostly she'd done it to make Colin laugh.

They were sitting on their own special sofa, eating cherries from the adults' drinks. All of the ladies in the first-class lounge were wearing fancy dresses and jewellery, and the men were smoking cigars. Sonia and Colin had a bad case of the giggles, but they were trying to keep quiet and listen to the captain.

"I just wanted to give you all an update on our position," the captain was saying. "Things are moving along quite well, but I do encourage you to keep your life jackets near at hand. We are not out of danger. U-boats patrol this area regularly. However, by this time tomorrow we will be in the American zone. The Germans won't interfere with any ship in neutral waters."

"So by tomorrow we'll all be safe?" asked a lady at the bar.

"Yes," said Captain Nicoll. "All being well, by tomorrow evening we'll be in the clear."

Sonia watched Colin spear a tiny cold sausage on a toothpick. "I guess that means you can take off your life jacket tomorrow night," she said.

"No," said Colin. "No, I promised my mum I'd wear it all of the time, until I walk down the gangplank and off the ship in Canada. I'm not going to break a promise."

Chapter Fifteen

TUESDAY, SEPTEMBER 17, 1940

On Tuesday morning, another storm rolled in. When Ken woke up he saw sleeting rain against the window of his cabin.

"Not again ..." Terry moaned on the bunk beneath him.

Ken looked out at the churning water, out to the horizon. Something was different.

He couldn't see the corvette that flanked their starboard side. Was it just below that trough of water? He watched the sea, waiting for it to reappear. He saw masts of one of the convoy freighters slipping in and out of view behind the waves. Where was the corvette?

He changed his position to look out toward the front of the convoy. The destroyer HMS *Winchelsea,* the lead ship of their defensive escort, was nowhere to be seen.

Ken dressed quickly and grabbed his overcoat. No one would miss him in the dining room. He headed to his lookout.

Lifeboat 12 had become his private hiding place, where no one could find him. He'd spent hours there yesterday, drawing his picture of the *Winchelsea*. It was a beautiful picture, with lots of detail. He was very proud of it. He was sure it would win the award.

He moved quickly and quietly across the rain-drenched deck and slid into the lifeboat, pulling the tarp carefully around him so that he could just see out a crack. He didn't mind the wet. The spray on his face was refreshing.

He stared ahead. It was true. The HMS *Winchelsea* was gone. And so were the two corvettes. What was going on? It didn't make sense to break up the convoy.

The SS *Marina* bobbed close by. He watched it sail up on the crest of each wave, and crash down into each trough. The winds were building. The rain was making it hard to see anything at all.

Suddenly, Ken heard voices nearby. He scrunched down onto the floor of the lifeboat.

"I tell you, they were havin' a real row. The captain, he says, 'We've got to cut loose now. With the escort gone, we've a better chance on our own,' he says."

Ken recognized the voice of Signalman Mayhew. He could smell a cigarette. The seaman must be on a break, having a smoke. He kept still, hidden under the covering of the lifeboat.

"I'm with the captain," said a second sailor, exhaling. "We're goin' too slowly, tryin' to keep pace with these freighters. This ship's got eighteen knots in her, and we're pokin' along, keepin' her at five. Easy pickin's for any U-boat."

"Well, you'll get no argument from the captain on that. Commodore Mackinnon, he says we've got to stay together 'til nightfall. He says no U-boat could launch a submerged attack in this weather. He says our danger is from a surface attack, and that the convoy will be better at spottin' for that." Mayhew sneezed violently. "Bloody rain."

Ken held onto his nose. The sneeze had made his nose itch, too. He tried to breathe slowly through his mouth.

"Well, they're not goin' to ask our opinion, whatever they do. Those two have been arguin' ever since we left port. I think," the sailor lowered his voice to a whisper, "I think that the commodore is tryin' to hang on to the convoy as long as he can because once it's gone, he's no longer in command. Here on the *Benares*, we're all under Captain Nicolls."

Signalman Mayhew snorted. "You might be right there. Who ever heard of a whole convoy doin' a zigzag? But that's what he's got us doin'. We may be able to avoid a surface attack, but we'll end up bashin' into each other to do it!"

Ken listened to the steps of the sailors as they headed back to their posts. He peeked out from under the tarp and looked out through the storm.

A surface attack meant he'd get a pretty good look at a U-boat.

* * *

Sonia kicked the door, deliberately scuffing her new shoe. Because of the stupid storm her mum had told her she had to play toy soldiers with Derek.

"Why me? Why can't Barbara?"

"Your sister isn't feeling well. The storm has got our tummies in a muddle. I need to have a rest and Derek needs distraction."

"Can I take him to the lounge?"

"No, you're to stay in your cabin with him. You made quite a mess during the last storm. The purser asked that you not go there again without supervision."

"How come Colin's allowed to go?"

"Colin is travelling on his own. And besides, he's got a stack of comics to read. He'll be quieter on his own."

"I can read comics, too!"

"Sonia! I said no. Now I am going to take a nap."

"My soldiers are going to shoot you down," Derek was

busy with his models from the Great War. He loved re-enacting the great battles. Sonia didn't know one battle from another, and didn't really care. She lay on her stomach on the floor and kicked the door.

Suddenly, there was a kick back. She jumped in surprise, and then went to open the door.

"Colin!" cried Derek. "You wanna play the battle of Passchendaele?"

"You weren't in the lounge, so I thought you might need some reinforcements." He brandished a cocktail glass filled with bright red sticky cherries. In the other hand he had a deck of cards. A stack of comics was tucked under his arm.

"Brilliant!" squealed Derek. "But Passchendaele first."

Sonia watched as Colin and Derek set up the soldiers. Derek kept a running commentary about the battle, and moved it along to its inevitable end. She lazily popped cherries into her mouth.

"Everyone's all a buzz in the lounge," said Colin, "because the destroyer's gone."

"Gone?" said Sonia. "What do you mean, gone?"

"The *Winchelsea* and the corvettes are gone from the convoy. It means we have no escort anymore."

"But we were promised the escort of the Royal Navy all of the way to Canada." Sonia frowned.

"They must have gone off to fight some Nazis," said Derek. "They don't wanna be hanging around with us when there are Nazis to fight!

"Mr. Nagorski—you know, the old Polish man—he said that we're in safe waters now. More than 650 miles out, and we're safe from U-boats. So we're clear all the way to Canada now. He even offered a cheer, toasting me and calling me 'Will Scarlet' ... 'cause of the life jacket, you know."

Sonia giggled. "Well, here's to Canada and Will Scarlet," she said, raising her glass of cherry stems in a toast. Colin blushed almost as red as his jacket.

* * *

Bess had spent most of the day in bed, fighting down her seasickness. But by teatime the storm had let up a bit and she weaved carefully up to the dining room. Beth, Joan, and Eleanor were there, sipping sweet tea and nibbling around the edges of pieces of dry toast. "The walking wounded," she waved and smiled weakly.

As the rain let up, more and more of the children made their way up to the dining room.

Patricia plunked down beside her. "Did you hear about the escort? They've gone. That must mean we're safe. The escort never left the *Volendam*. So we must be in neutral waters. Canada, here we come!"

Suddenly sunshine began to pour through the windows of the dining room. "All right, everyone, time for a bit of a walk," said Miss Day, "Time for some fresh air. Blow the stink off you," she said cheerfully as she herded them out to the sports deck.

"My mum always used to say that," said Beth. "'Blow the stink off ya.' I hope she isn't missing me too much."

"Look!" pointed Bess, "A rainbow!"

A huge rainbow stretched across the vast sky. With no land to restrict it, the rainbow seemed impossibly enormous and bright. Bess felt her spirits lift. She looked around her at the smiling faces, all of the children having come through a day of seasickness to a cup of tea and a beautiful rainbow. "It must be a good omen," she said.

Then she noticed Ramjam Buxoo walking among the children, seeking out the escorts one by one. Soon a buzz began to go through the groups.

Louis ran up to her. "Michael says we can sleep in pyjamas tonight! And we've got to have baths." After five days of sleeping in her clothes and kapok vest, Bess thought this sounded like sheer heaven.

"We must be in the clear!" Beth said to Bess. "We can stop worrying about torpedoes."

"We've left the war behind!" Bess hugged Beth and laughed with joy and relief. They danced a jig along the length of the sports deck as warm sea breezes lifted their skirts and the setting sun coloured their faces.

Chapter Sixteen

*W*HAM!

The explosion threw Ken out of his bunk, out of his dreams, into the dark, and onto the floor. He heard the sound of water rushing and was immediately wet. He stumbled up, feeling his way around the room. The alarm whistle was piercing his brain. A dim blue light was coming from where the door had been. There was now a gaping hole in the wall.

He knew the drill. He grabbed his kapok vest and life jacket and put them on over his pyjamas, shouting to Terry. "Let's go, Ter!" He tried to sound as cheery and as calm as possible, as though it was just like any other drill. He knew that this time it was not a drill.

"Aye, aye!" said Terry, as he grabbed his life jacket.

They waded into the corridor, cold water gushing over

their feet. Soft blue emergency lights gave everything an unreal glow. There was a sound of hissing steam. In the distance Ken could hear children calling out, some crying.

"It's the real thing, Ken!" Howard caught up to him as they headed toward their muster station in the playroom.

Suddenly Ken realized he'd forgotten his father's overcoat. *It'll be cold out there*, he thought. *We may have to sit in the lifeboat for a while.* And his stepmother had told him to take care of the coat. She'd be mad if he left it behind.

"Terry and Howard, you go on ahead to the playroom," he said, "I've got to go back."

"Wait," cried Terry, "I'll come too!"

"No," insisted Ken. "You go on ahead. I'll catch you up in a minute."

As Ken turned the corner toward his cabin, he heard an officer behind him shout to Terry and Howard, "Forget the muster station, boys. Go straight to your lifeboat on the embarkation deck."

Ken pushed through a stream of children going in the opposite direction. He made his way to his cabin and felt in the dark for his overcoat. He could hear water running everywhere. His hands fumbled with the straps as he took off his life jacket and his kapok vest. He put on his overcoat, then strapped on his kapok vest and his life jacket again. His heart was pounding. He wasn't afraid. He was excited! They'd been torpedoed!

He left his cabin and worked his way to the stairs, grateful for the warmth of the coat. There were lights flashing erratically. He heard odd zapping noises. He stretched to look over the line of children, to see what was ahead. As he turned a corner, he saw a huge gaping hole, the size of a football field. There were wires hanging out in every direction, and electric sparks flashing around the edges of the hole.

Ken was transfixed, and terrified. He turned his head away and let the slow moving queue of people push him through the dining room, toward the deck.

10:03 PM

"HELP! HELP! WE'RE TRAPPED!"

The heavy dresser had fallen, blocking the door of Bess's cabin. She put her glasses on, but could see no way out of the room. She tugged on her large green dressing gown and struggled to put her vest and life jacket over it. She and Patricia banged their fists against the wall. The dresser had made a jagged hole beside the door when it fell but the hole was small and high up. There was no way they could get through it.

"Help!" she screamed.

Suddenly, a large man's arm pushed through the hole. He smashed and punched at the wall, breaking away the plaster to make a bigger hole.

"Where are ya?" he called out.

"Here! We're beside the wall!"

The arm stretched and flailed through the hole. Bess grabbed it and it reached around her. The hand dug into her ribs, pulling her up and over the dresser and out into the corridor. The sailor set her down.

"There's another girl in there!"

He reached into the hole again. Bess could hear Patricia shrieking. "Over here! Over here!" The sailor grunted and strained and pulled Patricia out through the hole.

"You two, go. Get up the stairs. Forget your muster station. Get straight out on deck! Go!"

Bess and Patricia headed toward the stairway, just like in all of the drills. Except this time it was cold and dark and wet. There was water everywhere.

"Bess!" Bess wheeled around to see Beth, holding up her cabin mate Joan. Joan's legs were streaming with blood.

"Bess!" Joyce ran down the corridor from the other direction, crying and clutching her bear Winchell. She grabbed Bess.

"It's all right, Joyce," Bess worked to make her voice calm. "It's just like in the drills." She knelt down. "Patricia is going to take you to Auntie Mary. She'll be looking for you. I'm going to help Beth and Joan. We'll all meet up on deck." She passed Joyce's little hand over to Patricia.

"I'll let Miss Hillman know about Joan," said Patricia, calmly heading down the corridor.

Bess turned to Beth. She got on Joan's right side. "Can we

make a throne? Cross your wrists and clasp my hands. That's right. Now Joan, sit on our arms and grab our shoulders."

They lifted Joan and tried to walk forward, as other children pushed past them. It seemed to take forever to work their way down the hall. By the time they got to the stairwell, they were alone.

"Joan, you are going to have to crawl up. I don't think there is any way we can carry you," said Bess. Her heart was thumping.

CRRAAACKKK. There was a terrible wrenching noise. The stairs swayed back and forth.

"Look out!" screamed Beth, jumping backward. Bess yanked Joan out of the way just as the whole staircase collapsed. The three of them stared into the empty space above them.

"This can't be happening!" said Bess.

"Over here!" Cadet Haffner shouted to them from further up the corridor.

"We can't!" called Bess. "Joan's hurt!"

Cadet Haffner sprinted down the hall and heaved Joan over his shoulders. "Come this way," he grunted, leading them up the corridor to another set of stairs. Three flights up, and he opened the door to the embarkation deck.

The force of the storm hit Bess and Beth the minute they got on deck. The icy cold, the sleeting rain, and the deafening sound of wind. A couple of small girls were wandering around, looking bewildered. *Where is everyone?* thought Bess.

"Should we go back to the playroom?" she asked Cadet Haffner.

"No, everyone is to go straight to their boats. Which boat are you girls?" he said.

"Boat 5. Starboard side," Bess responded.

"Right. I'll get her over there. Then I've got to go back and check for others," he said, charging across the deck with Joan.

Bess and Beth followed Cadet Haffner to their lifeboat. The lascars had already removed the guardrail and lowered the lifeboat to the embarkation deck. They were standing there patiently, drenched to the skin in their thin cotton uniforms. The cadet set Joan down on the centre thwart and immediately headed back toward the stairs.

Patricia was there waiting for the order to board.

"Joyce is safe with Miss Cornish's group. She wanted to come with us, but I told her she had to go with her own group and that we'd see her on the rescue boat," Patricia said confidently. "We'll be picked up soon. You'll see. It'll be just like before, when the *Volendam* was hit. Fancy it happening again."

"Not to worry, girls," said Miss Hillman, as she arrived at the boat. "There are extra blankets on board. Once we're on, we'll wrap you up and have you warm in a jiffy."

Suddenly Bess went cold with fear. Louis! Where was

Louis?! Her mother had told her to look after him and now she didn't know where he was. How could she not know? There was chaos and cold and dark rain everywhere. She could hear waves crashing all around them. Where was her brother? Had he gotten to his boat safely?

As if reading her mind, Beth reached out and grasped Bess's hand. "I'm sure he's fine," she said softly. "He'll be with Michael. Michael can look after him."

They held hands, steadying themselves as the ship shuddered and rolled. "All right, in you go, girls," said one of the officers. Bess took a last look around the deck, hoping to see Louis. Behind the noise of the wind she could hear screams, cries for help, but she could see little in the dark sleet. Beth gently pulled her down beside her on the crowded side bench.

"Turns for lowering," the officer shouted.

Bess watched as the lascars began to unwind the heavy ropes, the falls as she remembered they were called, from the reel.

"Lower away!" shouted the officer.

The lascars began to play out the falls, inching the boat slowly down toward the churning water below. Suddenly, something caught. The front end plunged down and everyone in the boat jerked over. To Bess's horror, several lascar crewmen at the front end were hurled overboard into the sea.

"Noooooo!" Bess screamed. She dug her nails into the

gunwales. Then the back end of the boat fell and the boat hit the water with a smack. The lascars who had released the boat slid down on ropes from the deck and landed into the middle of the lifeboat.

"Knock open the slips," the officer called. Bess saw him release the boat rope and watched as the lifeboat worked itself free of the ship.

"Man the gears!" He yelled to the lascars to start working the Fleming gears and leapt over to join them, pushing and pulling with all his might.

"The *Benares* is going down! If we're too close we'll get sucked down with her. Move us away!" he yelled. Bess wasn't sure how much the lascars understood what he was saying, but she could see that they understood what he meant. They were pushing and pulling at the gears with all their might. She looked wildly around at the water, expecting to find the lascars who'd fallen out of the lifeboat. Surely they had to find them, rescue them. But they were nowhere to be seen amid the churning and swirling black water.

10:03 PM

In her cabin at the bow, Sonia was lying awake with a tummy ache. Too many cherries, she thought grumpily. Barbara had just turned off her reading light when Sonia felt the ship shudder. A distant alarm sounded.

"Oh," she said. She turned her light on, got out of bed, and began to put on her clothes, exactly as they had practiced it.

"Barbara. Barbara, wake up."

Barbara groaned. "Probably another drill ..."

"Doesn't matter," said Sonia nastily, "you've still got to get up and get dressed." Sonia already had on her skirt and stockings. She was struggling to put her vest on over her camel-hair coat, when her mother poked her head into the cabin.

"Oh, good, you're up. Right. Carry on." Sonia could see her brother Derek in his school uniform and cap, wearing his kapok vest and life jacket. Her mother was wearing her pearls, and carrying her handbag and jewellery box.

The four of them worked their way through the corridor to their muster station in the lounge. Sonia noticed a slight haze and an acrid smell in the air. The ship was quieter than usual. The usual *thump-thump* of the engines was silent. *Funny how you notice a sound when it stops*, she thought.

A couple of the other passengers looked up from their bridge game when Sonia's family walked in. She saw that the adults were still drinking cocktails. She checked her watch. It was ten fifteen. They probably hadn't been to bed yet.

"Anyone know what's going on?" her mother asked.

A man looked up from the couch where he was reading. "I think we might have hit some ship in the convoy. I heard one of the sailors talking earlier today and he said that was a danger—zigzagging in the dark."

Just then Colin came in, carrying his comic book collection. He was wearing his pyjamas, dressing gown, and slippers. He'd also put on some string gloves and a balaclava helmet. And of course he had on his own bright red kapok vest.

"Hail, Will Scarlet!" said Mr. Nagorski, laughing good-heartedly.

Colin leaned over to Sonia. "There was smoke in my corridor. It smells just like it did during the air raids," he said. "I think this is the real thing. I think we've been hit."

The bartender began mixing another round of cocktails. Colin looked at Sonia and quietly left the lounge.

Sonia sat down on the plush red sofa waiting patiently. She wondered if Colin was right. Had they really been hit? If they had been hit, shouldn't they go to their lifeboats?

Suddenly the lounge door flew open, bringing with it a gust of cold air. Officer Hetherington stared at all of them, sitting drinking, reading, and playing cards. "Oh, my God, you're all still here! Get to your boats! The ship is going down!"

10:20 PM

Ken was crossing the deck to his lifeboat, when a sailor stopped him. "All of those boats are gone now, son. You'll have to go over here." He pushed Ken into the queue to get onto lifeboat 12.

Ken was furious with himself. He'd missed his boat because of going back to get his coat. Exactly what the drills taught him not to do. Reverend King would be angry. He'd disobeyed orders.

He found himself a place to sit on the wooden side bench at the stern end of lifeboat 12. Well, at least it was *his* lifeboat, his lookout boat. Maybe it was meant to be, he thought to himself. He saw Howard and Derek beside him. Father O'Sullivan was here too, with a couple of little boys from his group. But most of the boat seemed to be filled with lascars. Ken recognized Ramjam Buxoo among them.

Cadet Haffner came running up with a boy over one shoulder. "The other boats are gone," he puffed, as he threw the boy into the boat on top of Father O' Sullivan. It was Fred. Ken and Derek pushed over to make room and they huddled in the stern.

The lifeboat swayed precariously. The wind and rain was picking up. The ocean seemed to be moving away from them. Ken realized the *Benares* was starting to roll. They were getting hoisted up in the air, further away from the sea.

A man with a shiny black hat and stylish coat was shouting to the officer over the roar of the storm. "I'm concerned that not all of the children have made it up to the deck, Officer Cooper. We can't leave yet."

"The ship is listing badly, Mr. Nagorski" said Officer Cooper. "We've searched everywhere."

"But there are more boys who are supposed to be in this lifeboat with us," said Father O'Sullivan weakly. "I'm sure they must be on their way."

"We've checked below deck for missing children," said Officer Cooper. "There's no one. We've very little time left."

A steward was directing Miss Cornish—Auntie Mary—into their lifeboat. She looked very upset.

"But my girls! I've sworn to look after them," she said as Officer Cooper tried to persuade her into the boat.

"It's all right, miss," he said, "They've already gone ahead in other lifeboats. We need you to come in this one with us."

"But Joyce will be frightened! She's the littlest. She didn't meet me in the muster station, and I haven't been able to find her anywhere on deck." Auntie Mary sounded frantic. "I need to check the muster station again!"

The steward turned to Officer Cooper. "All of the muster stations are clear, sir. There is no one else waiting."

"Thank you, Mr. Purvis." Officer Cooper turned to Miss Cornish. "Joyce is obviously with one of the other groups. I am sure she is safe. We must leave the ship. Now." He turned to the lascars holding the handles. "Turns for lowering."

Ken gripped the side of the boat as it swung wildly in the wind. Mr. Nagorski took Auntie Mary by the elbow and moved to guide her down into the boat. "Miss Cornish, it is time to save your life. And we'll all need your help on this boat."

She looked down at Ken and the other boys in the boat.

She grasped Mr. Nagorski's hand and stepped off the deck of the *Benares* and into the lifeboat. As Mr. Nagorski and Steward Purvis followed her into the boat, Officer Cooper shouted the orders: "Start the falls!"

The lifeboat began to drop away from the deck. There was a sudden lurch. The stern end dropped. Auntie Mary shrieked. Ken fell backward. He heard a scream and thought he saw a body falling through the air, from the end of their boat to the water below.

He held on with all his strength. The bow jerked down. Now the boat was level, although with the *Benares* at such an angle, and the water below rising and falling, Ken found it hard to make sense of anything.

The noise was deafening: the howling wind, the smashing of the waves, and through it all the sound of screaming.

They hit the water with a hard *thwack* and immediately rose on the crest of a wave. Then the boat slid down into a trough. Looking up, Ken saw four terrified lascars, yelling as they slid down the launching ropes toward the lifeboat. Officer Cooper held the painter, keeping the boat as close to the ship as he could. The lascars let go about ten feet above the lifeboat and dropped in, falling on top of the other crewmen.

"Knock free the falls," Officer Cooper yelled above the howl of the wind. He and Steward Purvis simultaneously knocked open slips at either end of the boat and Ken felt the water pull the boat away from the ship. He saw Officer Cooper release the painter. They were free of the *Benares*.

"Purvis—get onto the Fleming gears. Buxoo, get your men working. We've got to pull away from the ship," he shouted. The lascars and crew pulled and pushed together, moving the boat out into the sea.

10:20 PM

The fierce wind of the storm made Sonia want to turn back to the comfort of the lounge. But she went with her mother, sister, and brother to lifeboat 4, as she had done at every drill, every day.

But this time, in the dark, with a storm raging all around, it was terrifying. There were children everywhere. Sonia had no idea there were so many children on board. They were wandering around in pyjamas, clutching teddy bears and dolls, holding life jackets limply by their sides. She saw a girl about Barbara's age, kneeling, her arms wrapped around four crying brothers and sisters. She saw a nurse holding a girl. They were both covered in blood. A small child held a large teddy bear. Fleeting images, as her mother's iron grip pulled her quickly forward toward their lifeboat.

Then, Sonia's heart skipped a beat. Their lifeboat wasn't there. The lascars were turning the handles and reeling out the ropes and as she looked down over the edge, she could just make out their lifeboat dangling beside the ship, almost at the water.

"Wait! Stop!" her mother cried.

A sailor turned to them, his white face stricken. "I can't! We can't reel the boat back up—it's too heavy."

"But what do we do now? We're supposed to be in that boat!" shrieked Sonia's mother.

"Do you think you can you climb down on a rope?" the sailor asked. "This one, the painter, is connected directly to the front of the lifeboat"

Sonia was stunned. Her mother stared, open-mouthed. The lascars stood stiffly holding the handles that connected the ropes to the lifeboat far below.

"Yes," said Barbara, suddenly. "Yes, I can. I did it at school, mother," she said as her mother started to object. "I'll go first, and you'll see how easy it is." She grabbed the painter as the sailor held it steady. She worked her way off of the open deck and began to inch down, hand over hand.

Sonia stared down into the dark and mist. She could barely see the lifeboat below. It was as though Barbara had launched herself into the vast unknown. But then she heard a thump and a cheer. Barbara had landed safely.

"Come on then, young lad, I'll take you down meself," said one of the other sailors. He grabbed the rope and placed Derek in front of him. "Hold on tight. That's right. Just one hand at a time," he said. "We'll go together."

Derek's eyes were full of concentration as they headed down into the mist below. Suddenly the sailor holding the top of the rope swore.

"What?! What?!" screamed Sonia's mother. Her voice sounded thin over the roar of the wind.

"The lifeboat is moving away," he shouted. "A wave hit them and pulled them from the ship. It must have wrenched the painter loose. Your son is on his way back up."

"But what about Barbara!" wailed Sonia's mother.

"She's in good hands. Officer Macrae is there, commanding the lifeboat. She's safe with him."

Derek's eyes were wide with fear and excitement when he got back to the deck of the ship. "It was like flying. We were just hanging from the rope and the wind was blowing us all around."

Sonia turned around to look at the embarkation deck. Everywhere there were people running and falling, screaming, and crying. The ship lurched and she lost her balance and fell. The ship's bow started to rise into the air and she started to slide.

"Grab the rail!" her mother shouted. Sonia held on as the cold spray from a wave hit her.

"I need my hands free," her mother shouted. "I'm not going to be able to carry my purse, but we can't lose our money." Sonia watched her mother frantically shove money and passports into her pockets.

"Sonia, put my jewellery in your pockets." But as her mother opened her jewellery box there was a jolt, and rings, pearls, earrings, and necklaces scattered on the deck. Her mother screamed and dropped to her knees trying to gather up the gems.

Suddenly the ship lurched again, and all three of them fell sideways. Sonia landed flat on the icy deck. She pulled her sopping hair out of her eyes and looked around, trying to figure out what to do. She got on her knees and scanned the embarkation deck. The sailors were gone. The lascars were gone.

All of the lifeboats were gone.

Sonia felt nauseous as panic began to overtake her.

"Down here!" A strong voice reached them in the darkness. "To the stern! To the rafts!"

Sonia slid downhill with Derek and her mother to the stern end of the ship. Officer Hetherington and Mr. Davis, the man from the BBC, were untying flat wooden rafts and pushing them out into the water. The rafts looked like a bunch of rugged dining tables, bobbing on the waves.

BOOOOOM! A huge explosion made Sonia's heart jump.

"Probably the boiler," yelled Mr. Davis above the roar.

Sonia looked back toward the bow of the ship. It was high in the air now. She saw her mother gripping Derek with one hand and clenching the deck rail with the other. Her eyes were fixed on the water that was inching ever closer.

"Here! Down here!" A voice called to them from the water. Sonia looked over the edge. A young sailor was swimming about ten feet below them, holding onto a raft.

"You've got to jump. Jump onto the raft. Hurry!"

Sonia turned to look into her mother's eyes. "Go," her mother said. "Go now. Show your brother how."

Sonia squeezed through the railing and stood on the edge of the ship. Spray from the waves drenched and temporarily blinded her. She took a deep breath. Her heart pounded. She let go of the rail and jumped.

10:33 PM

The *Benares* was almost vertical now. The bow was sticking high up in the air.

The moon came out from behind a cloud and suddenly, briefly, Bess saw the water around them filled with bits and pieces from the ship. Deck chairs floated by. A suitcase bobbed along. A linen napkin from the dining room floated on top of the waves. And there were people. Swimming, thrashing, screaming. In the water. So many people in the water.

The lights on the ship shone intensely in the darkness. They seemed impossibly bright. *Like a Christmas tree with all the lights on*, thought Bess, as she clung to lifeboat 5.

All of that lovely food, thought Sonia, wet through, clinging to the raft. *All of that ice cream.*

It's like a living thing, thought Ken in lifeboat 12. "It was our home," he heard Howard say softly beside him.

As the ship slid down into the water, they all heard a sound like a huge groan.

With that, the *Benares* was gone.

Chapter Seventeen

For a second, a sliver of moonlight showed what looked like a huge hole that the *Benares* left in the ocean. Another second and Bess saw the hole rise up as a thirty-foot tidal wave. It was on top of her before she could react.

She was flipped backward into the icy black sea. The intense cold stopped all thoughts. Her thick green dressing gown, which had kept her warm moments before, was as heavy as lead, pulling her down. She thrashed frantically, grabbing at the air, grabbing at the water, terrified by the violent waves.

But suddenly she heard her father's voice in her head. He had taught her how to swim two summers ago.

"Your life jacket will hold you up, Bessie. You just have to relax. Don't fight the water," she heard him say.

She felt another wave crash above her, pushing her

further down, twisting her until she had no sense of up or down. She calmed herself and stayed still. A moment later she popped up to the surface.

She took in a huge breath of the frigid air. She looked up and saw the lifeboat ahead of her. She pulled the water with her arms, swimming just the way her father had shown her. It was hard—the life jacket made her movements clumsy and awkward. Her dressing gown pulled her down. The sea pushed her backward as she struggled to reach the boat.

Her father's voice rang in her ears. "Stroke, breathe, stroke, breathe." Slowly, she got to the side of the boat. It was half submerged, barely floating. But she pulled herself up and lay on the gunwale, one leg in the boat, the other over the edge in the sea.

A cloud covered the moon. It was pitch black. The sound of rain and waves filled everything. Bess strained her eyes. Miraculously, her glasses were still on. She saw movement in the water, close by.

"Beth! Over here!" Bess called, the wind whipping her voice away.

Beth was struggling. She clearly was not a swimmer, but her life jacket was keeping her head above the water. A wave rose and she disappeared. Bess felt her heart lurch. The next moment, Beth popped up to the surface again.

As Bess kept her eyes glued on Beth, she was aware of other people thrashing toward the boat and grabbing hold.

She felt like she was willing Beth over, pulling her with her eyes. Suddenly, a wave rose and Beth disappeared.

Bess held her breath and counted. One. Two. Three. Four. Five seconds—how long could a person hold their breath under water?

Suddenly Beth's head popped up, gasping, only a few feet from Bess.

"Beth! Here! Grab hold!"

The lifeboat listed to the side as Beth grabbed the edge and awkwardly pulled herself up. There were ten or twelve adults clinging along the side, but Bess couldn't see anyone she knew. Where was Miss Hillman? Where were Patricia and Joan? Where were Gussie, Connie, and Violet?

Beth was breathing hard beside her. Her life jacket was shimmering, as though covered in sequins. *How odd*, thought Bess. *Has the cold damaged my eyes?* She looked down and saw her own jacket glowing. Plankton, she realized. She vaguely remembered learning about phosphorescent plankton in science class. *How strange the things that come into your head*, she thought. *It would be pretty, if it weren't so awful.* It all felt so unreal.

Then without warning, another huge wave hit the side of the boat and Bess was tossed into the sea again.

She was completely disoriented. There was water above and water below. She didn't know which way was up. It was so dark. And so terribly cold. She worked to relax, and as she did, her head bobbed above the surface of the water.

She gulped at the air and choked on salt spray.

The lifeboat was over to her left. It had completely flipped over. She swam toward it, aware of others heading in the same direction. She stretched and pulled herself up, grabbed the keel, and lay spread out on the hull of the boat. Beth was there, across from her, on the other side of the overturned boat.

"Are you all right?" Bess could see Beth's hands clenched onto the keel.

"Yes," Beth said faintly.

Rescue would come soon. The other boats in the convoy would come to pick them up any minute. If they could just hold onto the boat, they'd be saved.

But Louis. What about Louis? What if his boat had tipped too? He couldn't swim as well as she could. Was he struggling somewhere out there right now?

Further along the keel of the boat, Bess saw other pairs of hands, one covered in large gem-studded rings, clinging on just like her. Waiting. Waiting in the dark. Praying for rescue.

Her dressing gown pressed her onto the hull. But at least it protected her a bit from the vicious wind and stinging hail. She stretched her head up as high as she could to try and see a rescue ship. But she could see nothing, except occasional flashes of phosphorescence.

The darkness consumed her, the cold burned. What if Louis was lost? How could she go back home to her parents without him? How could she possibly tell her mother that she lost Louis in the sea?

* * *

Sonia's hands gripped the wooden slats. It took all of her concentration just to hold onto the raft. The slats had spaces between them, only large enough for her fingers. But the ropes holding the raft were loose. The slats kept moving and squishing her hands. Nothing felt firm.

She lay face down, staring through the spaces at the oil drums below. Two empty oil drums for buoyancy held together by rope and a few pieces of wood. It seemed so little between her and the endless ocean.

Her mother was in the middle of the raft lying on top of Derek, holding him down to make sure he didn't slip off. He looked so small, his tiny bare legs sticking out under the short trousers of his school uniform. The sailor who had helped them onto the raft was on the other side. Mr. Davis had stayed with them long enough to get them away from the *Benares* but then swam away to help people on another raft. Now he was nowhere in sight. There were just the four of them, lying on a raft about the size of a small dining table. She wished she was in the boat with Barbara. Or in whichever boat Colin was. Anywhere, anything would be better than this raft.

Sonia couldn't tell if it was raining, hailing, or just spraying water. The raft soared up to the top of each wave and then came smashing down, slamming their bodies with the impact. She was drenched through and cold, so horribly cold.

The sound of the crashing waves filled every part of her mind. There was a brief moment of quiet when they rode the crest of a wave, but it was only a short respite from the pounding of the water. With each wave, the buoyancy drums shifted and the slats squeezed and crushed her fingers.

Why was no one coming to rescue them?

Sonia had a horrifying thought. What if no one knew where they were? What if no one was able to see them in this pitch black night?

The effort of holding on was almost impossible. She was tired, so terribly, terribly tired.

Sonia felt her fingers begin to relax their grip. She felt calm as her body slid slowly off the raft and into the ocean.

White water. Rushing toward her. Let it come. It was a dream. She was warm. She was safe.

Suddenly, she was wrenched back to cold and consciousness. She was face down on the raft. The young sailor was pressing on her back, trying to push water out of her lungs. She was awake and terribly frightened.

"Don't you go doin' that again!" he yelled at her. "I might not be able to get you next time. You just hold onto the side here, like a good girl."

Sonia looked over at her mother. Her mother's eyes were wild. Sonia watched her pry one of her bloodied hands off the raft and pull a small flask out of her pocket. She passed it to the sailor. "Make her drink a sip of this," she croaked.

The sailor took the flask, opened it and put it to Sonia's lips. She took a small sip and coughed violently. It burned her mouth and throat. He passed the flask back to her mother.

"What is your name?" her mother asked.

"Tommy, ma'am," he said. "Tommy Milligan."

"Please ... have some, Tommy," her mother said.

Tommy took a large sip and passed the flask back to her mother. "Thank you, ma'am. Much appreciated." Her mother took some herself.

"We'll save some for later," she said, lying her head back on top of Derek.

The drink made Sonia feel warm on the inside, momentarily. But then her body seized up with the cold. Her legs were cramping. She wished she could kneel or sit up. But it was impossible. There was no way to stay steady on the raft.

Icy water crashed down on them from the sky and from the sea. Had hours passed? She had no way of knowing. The blackness was everywhere. The noise of the waves and wind blocked out thought. The cold was unbearable.

She realized that she desperately needed to pee. Such

an ordinary thing, but here? On a raft in the middle of the Atlantic Ocean? There was nothing she could do—she had to relax where she was, spread-eagled on the raft, and let go. She felt the warmth of her urine spread through her stockings. It wasn't disgusting. It was wonderful. She was so thankful for just that bit of warm. Until the next wave washed it all away and she was left cold again.

Sonia was trying to stay awake as Tommy had told her to, but it was hard. Her mind seemed to move in slow motion. She thought about Barbara. Had she been pitched into the sea, or was she still on that lifeboat? Was she swimming in the ocean, or warm in a nice soft bed? A nice soft bed. Sonia started to imagine herself in a bed, her head on a huge fluffy pillow.

"Sonia, dear," Her mother's voice sounded very far away. "I think maybe we should just take off our life jackets ... and go to sleep in the sea ..." she said slowly.

Sonia jolted out of her exhaustion. "No!" she shouted. "No, mother, we can't do that! Derek! Shake mum! Derek, wake up!"

Sonia heard Derek mumble. He was still lying underneath her mother.

"You have to hang on, Mother. Mother!?"

"Yes, dear?" her mother sounded as though she was talking in her sleep.

"It'll be light soon. We'll be rescued soon." Sonia was

furious with her mother. "You have to wake up! Tommy, don't let her sleep!"

Her anger felt good. It warmed her up. She reached out and tried to hit her mother. She accidentally smacked Derek's bare leg.

"Ow!" Derek started to cry.

"It's all right, she didn't mean it," said her mother.

They were not going to die out here in the ocean. She was sure of that. But they had to stay awake and alert, keep watching for rescue, and not give up.

* * *

Lifeboat 12 was very full. Ken was squashed into the bow with the other boys. Auntie Mary and Father O'Sullivan were beside him. Father O'Sullivan looked faint. His head nodded onto his chest.

In the middle of the boat, Mr. Purvis and seven of the lascars were pulling and pushing on the Fleming gears. On either side of them were more lascars—about thirty of them, Ken thought—looking very cold, miserable, and bewildered.

A wave raised the boat up into the air and Ken looked down into a cavern of water below. Just as quickly, the boat slid down the water, and Ken looked up at a wave as high as a mountain towering above him. Up and down, like a ride at a fun fair. It was scary, but it was also pretty exciting. But then again, he was safely in a boat. He was aware that all around him people were thrashing in the water.

With the *Benares* gone, there was less urgency to move away. Officer Cooper steered toward one of the swimmers. Ken watched Ramjam and Mr. Purvis pull in a crewman he immediately recognized as Cadet Critchley, from their first day on the boat. Then they pulled in another crewman—the signalman, Johnny Mayhew.

Suddenly, a hand reached up from the water and grabbed onto the gunwale right beside him. Ken screamed. The boat tipped to the side as Harry Peard, the gunner who had spit on the seagull, pulled himself in. He stood up on the side bench beside Ken and shook himself off— *like a dog shaking off water*, Ken thought as the water splattered him.

The lifeboat was now *very* full. People were sitting on the side benches, on the gunwales, on the thwarts, on the bottom of the boat. There clearly wouldn't be room for any others. *I'm sure another boat will pick them up*, thought Ken.

Officer Cooper shouted above the roar of the storm. "Rescue will be here soon. But we need to keep the boat moving. I am going to need everyone to take turns working the Fleming gears."

Peard growled to Ken. "Come on. Let's see what yer made of."

"Aye, aye, sir!" said Ken. He squeezed through the lascars

to get into position. Watching Peard, Ken pushed and pulled the lever in front of him. He felt the propeller shaft turning. He could feel the boat moving. But since it was also going up and down in the waves, it was hard to tell what direction they were heading.

"Roll out the barrel, and we'll have a barrel of fun!" a voice sang out.

Ken wasn't sure who started the song, but soon he was singing at the top of his lungs. *It* was *a barrel of fun*, thought Ken. It was the best adventure imaginable. He imagined the captain of the Royal Navy, maybe even Prime Minister Churchill himself, bringing a rescue destroyer alongside them. Everyone would be amazed at his strength and valour. It would be glorious. There would be pictures and stories in the paper.

"Zing boom tararrel. Ring out a song of good cheer. Now's the time to roll out the barrel, for the gang's all here!"

But after he sang "Roll out the Barrel" six times, "Pack up Your Troubles" four times, and went through one hundred bottles of beer in "Ninety-nine Bottles of Beer on the Wall," Ken was exhausted, cold, and drenched to the skin. He let Howard have a turn with the Fleming gears while he sat, catching his breath in the bow. One of the lascars was busy with the bailing bucket, trying to keep the worst of the sea spray and rain out of the bottom of the boat. There was still no sign of the Royal Navy.

The boat didn't really seem to be moving anywhere. It rose and fell on the waves, but it was impossible to get a sense of any progress. Then again what, Ken wondered, was progress? Where were they trying to go? Were they just moving the handles to stay warm and to keep the boat from flipping over?

Suddenly, Johnny Mayhew shouted over the roar of the wind. "A light!"

"It's a rescue ship!" said Fred. Ken strained his eyes to see. Officer Cooper steered their boat toward the light. The crew on the Fleming gears pulled and pushed harder than ever.

Doesn't look like a rescue vessel, thought Ken. It's smaller than us.

"Ahoy," called Officer Cooper.

"Ahoy," came a response. "What ship are you?"

"The *City of Benares*," Officer Cooper responded. "And you?"

"SS *Marina*," said the voice. "Captain Paine at the helm"

Ken remembered the *Marina* in convoy with them. He'd drawn her in port.

"So it's true," Howard leaned over to Ken. "The *Marina* was torpedoed, too. I overheard Peard say it to Officer Cooper."

"But the *Marina* was one of the ships that was supposed to look after us!" said Ken.

Officer Cooper brought their boat alongside the *Marina*'s

lifeboat. He threw a rope across to loosely lash the boats together. Ken could see two sailors holding torches. That was the light they'd seen: torches looking in the water for survivors.

"We'll have a better chance of being found if we stay together," Captain Paine said. "I'm sure a rescue vessel will be here in the morning."

In the morning? Ken looked at the other boys, shivering in the cold sleet and hail. *It's lucky I went back for my overcoat after all*, he thought. *I'd be in really bad shape if I were only in pyjamas.* He looked across to the lascars, sitting stiffly in the middle of the boat in their light cotton uniforms. He hoped daylight would come soon and bring some warm sunshine with it.

Chapter Eighteen

WEDNESDAY, SEPTEMBER 18, 1940, 1:00 AM

Bess had no idea how long it had been since the *Benares* had gone down. Hail was battering her head and arms on the overturned lifeboat. The ice made it impossible to keep a hold on the keel. The boat rode the crest of a wave, and as it smacked down, she saw Beth lose her grip and begin to slide away.

"No! Beth!" Bess was terrified of letting go, but she was equally terrified of losing Beth. She inched her way to the end of the boat and, holding the keel with one hand, frantically grabbed at the water. Beth was off the boat now, and moving away from her.

Suddenly, Bess's hand hit a rope lying across the hull. It was attached to the stern. It was so thick that she could barely close her fingers around it. But she managed to thrust it toward Beth.

"Grab onto the rope," she cried to Beth. "Grab on! Never let go!"

She felt Beth's grip on the other end. The rope tightened as Beth used all her strength to pull herself back onto the boat.

"Wind it around your wrists," said Bess. They were now facing each other, sprawled over the rounded hull of the boat, their toes touching the edge of the gunwale. They entwined their hands together in the rough rope. Their weight was balanced on either side of the hull. Their fingers were relieved from the difficult task of holding onto the keel. They were securely fastened.

Bess looked along the edge of the keel. There were no other hands on the boat.

They were alone.

It was the darkest part of the night. The storm was fully overhead. Hail hit her arms like gravel. Ice chunks collected at the back of her neck. With each wave the boat went up and then crashed down. There was a terrible moment at the top of the wave when the boat fell to the sea and they were suspended in the air, tethered only by the rope twisting into their flesh. The next instant their bodies smashed onto the hull.

"Beth? Are you all right?" Bess called weakly. Her throat was raw from saltwater.

"Yes. Mostly. You?"

Yes, she was all right. She was bruised and sore and wet

throughout, but she was alive. They'd gotten to this boat together and they would make it through, together. They just had to hang on.

There was no moon. They were in complete dark and intense cold. Bess kept looking for a light from a rescue ship. But there was nothing—nothing but the rise and fall of the boat, the slamming of their bodies into the hull, the slapping of the waves over their bodies.

"They'll be able to see us in the morning." Bess croaked. Talking was hard. Whenever she tried to say more than a word or two, salty seawater slammed into her mouth, choking her.

"I've got ... I've got to ... make it ... for my mother," said Beth.

Bess thought about Louis. *I've got to make it so I can explain everything to Mum and Dad,* Bess thought. *They've lost their only son. I have to survive. To tell them.*

"We can do this," she said. "We just have to stick together."

Up and down. Their hands were locked in position on the rope. The waves crashed over them.

"All right, Bess?"

"Yes. All right, Beth?"

"Yes."

On and on, wave after wave.

"That was a rough one."

"Yes, rough one."

Minute after minute.

Rise. Fly. Fall. Smash. Rise. Fly. Fall. Smash.

Hour after hour.

"It'll be ... light soon."

"Yes ... they'll ... see us ..."

Up and down.

A fish ... flying ...

A plate of food drifting toward her.

School was just starting. Bess was racing toward her desk. She was so happy to see everyone. She'd come out of the bomb shelter. No one was hurt. No more bombs.

There was the rocking horse from the playroom.

And here was Taffy, jumping up and licking her nose. There must be a stick around here somewhere that she could throw for him.

What's that?

Something has changed, thought Bess. Something is different.

She turned her head slowly. There was a light in the distance. It was the sun coming up.

She was clinging onto the hull of an overturned boat in the middle of the ocean.

She turned to look at her friend. Beth was looking at her.

"They'll see us now ..." she whispered.

As the sun rose, the wind and the waves died down. The rain slowed to a drizzle. The boat rocked gently beneath them.

Bess lifted her head and looked around for the other lifeboats.

There was nothing. Nobody. In the vastness of the ocean, with only water as far as the eye could see, they were all alone.

It was impossible. There had been more than four hundred people on the ship. Where were they all?

The sky lightened and became a chalky grey as the sun inched its way above the horizon. The bright orange light blinded her and Bess turned her head away.

With the movement of the sun she understood the passage of time. The sun rose above the ocean as the sky shifted to pale blue. Bess's eyes were puffy and swollen, her glasses encrusted with salt. She could see nothing clearly. Once, she thought she saw a lifeboat filled with people coming toward them. But it drifted away without a word, like a dream.

She listened to the sound of her breath. It was the only sound she could hear. She couldn't feel her hands or feet.

Chapter Nineteen

WEDNESDAY, SEPTEMBER 18, 1940, 4:30 AM

Sonia looked out over the black sea. It was getting lighter. The rain had stopped. The sea was calm. Soon they'd be able to see other rafts and lifeboats.

But as the dawn rose, the terrible truth struck. They were alone. Nothing but water in every direction.

Sonia looked down through the slats to the water below. The ropes that held the raft together were fraying, loosening with each successive wave.

She looked at her brother, pinned under her mother. His school cap was long gone, and his uniform was ripped. Her mother's face was scratched and puffy. Her hand was searching in her pocket for her flask. It came out empty. "It must have fallen out in the night," she murmured.

Tommy Milligan stretched his head up and scanned the horizon.

"There," he pointed, "there's a mast."

Sonia could see nothing but a large wave coming at them. She held her breath as it crashed over her. She shook the water from her face and looked again. They were riding to the top of the wave. *Was* that a mast in the distance?

The waves pushed them up and down maddeningly, hiding and revealing ... yes! A tiny sail on a tiny mast. A sail? Sonia didn't know much about boats, but she knew this didn't look like a rescue ship.

Tommy steadied himself with one hand on the edge of the raft. Sonia watched him take off his sopping shirt. He stretched up as high as he could, still holding the raft's edge. His arm waved the wet rag of a shirt. Would the boat see them? Each time the sea pushed them up, Tommy waved. Each time they crashed down, he gripped the edge of the raft.

They waited. It was agonizing. But the mast seemed to be getting bigger. Yes, definitely. The boat was coming toward them. Gradually, the distance between them closed.

"Ahoy," someone shouted to them. "Are you from the *Benares*?"

"Yes, sir," Tommy Milligan's voice sounded strong. "I have three passengers with me, sir. Two are children."

The boat had dropped its sail. Sailors were rowing steadily toward them.

"Commanding Officer Lewis, here. We're from the SS *Marina*. We'll get you in here with us in a jiffy."

Sonia was bewildered. Clearly this was just a tiny lifeboat, much smaller than the lifeboats from the *Benares*. There were only about ten men in it and it looked full. Was this the rescue boat? Were they taking them to the SS *Marina*?

A sailor threw a towrope across to Tommy. He caught it and pulled the raft toward the lifeboat. He looped the rope around the end of one of the raft's planks and made them fast.

Tommy reached over, quickly scooped Derek up in his arms and passed him across to the waiting arms of one of the lifeboat's sailors.

He turned to Sonia. Sonia wasn't sure she could stand on her own. She was rigid and shaking violently. He picked her up as though she weighed no more than a doll, and gently passed her into the lifeboat.

"Ma'am?" Sonia's mother seemed frozen to her spot. "May I help you into the lifeboat?" Tommy asked gingerly. Her mother gave the smallest of nods. Sonia wasn't sure that her mother understood what was happening.

"We'll just wait for this wave to pass," said Tommy, reassuringly. A wave pushed the raft and the lifeboat high into the air. As they fell, they went down at different speeds. It looked like the raft would break off from the boat. Sonia screamed as the wave crashed over Tommy and her mother. But as the water receded, Tommy was calmly lifting her mother up and passing her into the waiting arms of Officer Lewis.

Although he wasn't much older than her sister Barbara, Sonia thought Tommy Milligan was the strongest man she had ever seen. He stepped into the lifeboat and the sailors cut the towrope. Sonia watched their little raft float away into the distance. It looked so small.

"Probably wouldn't have lasted another hour," she heard Officer Lewis say to Tommy. "Here, miss," he said, turning to Sonia, "We've got a dry blanket for you, and a tot of rum."

"Oh, please, no more rum!" Sonia blurted out, remembering the burning taste from her mother's flask. Tommy and all of the sailors laughed. "Well, we've got a bit of condensed milk for you then. You need to drink it to keep up your strength. And here's a couple of ship's biscuits."

Sonia watched her mother and Tommy gratefully accept the rum. Her mother gave a drop to Derek, who was curled up on the bottom of the boat beside her. He coughed and clutched his mother.

Sonia took a sip of the milk, and a small bite of a biscuit, but found it hard to swallow. She couldn't stop shivering underneath the rough blanket. She leaned on the other side of her mother.

The sailors hoisted up the mast and the boat began to move forward on the wind.

"Have you seen any lifeboats from the *Benares*?" Sonia's mother asked. Sonia knew she was thinking about Barbara.

The officer shook his head. "We haven't. We were about a mile away from the *Benares* when it went down. We're from the SS *Marina*, one of the merchant ships in the convoy."

"Are you taking us to the *Marina*?" asked Sonia's mother.

"The *Marina* was hit. It sank right after the *Benares* went down. The crew all made it safely to our two lifeboats."

"Where is the other one?" asked Sonia's mother.

"We haven't seen it since we launched."

Sonia's mother looked around the vast extent of the ocean. "Where are all of the convoy boats? There were eighteen ships all together. Where are they?"

"Well, ma'am, it's complicated. There are rules. When a boat is torpedoed, all of the other ships in the convoy have the order to disperse."

"What? You mean they all left us?"

There was a silence as the sailors looked at each other.

"You mean they left us to drown?!"

"Ma'am, they had to follow orders. Orders are to leave the area immediately because once a U-boat is firing at a convoy they will take down as many as they possibly can. It got the two of us—it would have gotten more, given a chance," Officer Lewis explained.

"But why didn't you fight back?" Her mother's eyes were blazing.

"None of the convoy ships would have a chance against a U-boat. The destroyer is the one with the guns to take on a U-boat."

"But where was the destroyer? Where the hell was the

Winchelsea? Why did it leave us yesterday morning?" Sonia's mother was yelling.

"I can only say that the commodore must have thought we were in safe water, ma'am. This is supposed to be neutral territory. This is further out than any U-boat has ever struck before. Up until now they haven't been able to get this far from shore without refuelling," he said. "It was a surprise to us all."

Sonia's mother was quiet. She looked around at the empty vast ocean. "But where are the other lifeboats? My daughter was on a lifeboat. They said she'd be safe."

"I'm sure she is, ma'am. If she is in a lifeboat, she'll be well looked after."

Sonia's mother rocked Derek. "What happens now? Where are you taking us?"

"We are heading for Ireland," said the officer.

"Ireland!" gasped Sonia's mother.

"Yes, ma'am. By my estimation it will take us six days to get there."

Sonia's heart sank. She looked at her mother's grim face, her hair frizzed around her head like a misshapen halo. Sonia felt her own hair. Her tight plaits had unraveled. She looked down at her lovely camel-hair coat, covered with black, greasy oil. Her brother was tucked in tight beside her mother, his uniform shredded. His eyes rolled as he fell asleep.

Six days in this tiny boat?

Suddenly, Tommy shouted, "A raft! Portside!"

Officer Lewis loosened the sail and directed the crew to man the oars. Sonia strained her eyes to see what Tommy had seen, but her lids were swollen and painful. She saw her mother stand to look, clearly hoping that it might be Barbara. But as they drew up to the tiny wooden structure she saw only two weak lascar crewmen.

The crew of the *Marina* lifeboat guided the shivering lascars into their lifeboat. Sonia counted fifteen in the boat. There wasn't another inch of room. Her bent knees were pressing into the back of the lascar in front of her. How they could possibly last a week? There was no room to lie down, and no toilet. How on earth would they manage?

The sun was now almost directly overhead. The warmth of it began to relax her body. There was a good breeze and Sonia could feel the boat grab onto the wind as they set the sail. The reflection of the sun off the water hurt her eyes. Wrapped in a blanket, her stomach rumbling with the thick coating of condensed milk, she began to doze.

In a dream state Sonia heard the distant sound of a siren. She wondered where the nearest air-raid shelter was. She tried to start running, but her legs didn't work.

"It's a destroyer! Come to!"

The words crashed into her mind. She opened her eyes to see a sailor madly waving a makeshift flag, a shirt tied to an oar. She could see a ship in the distance, but then it dipped behind the swell of the ocean. There it was again. Now it was gone. Was it real? Had it seen them? Could this actually be rescue?

She heard the siren blare again.

The ocean moved and she could see the ship again.

It was closer. It was definitely closer.

It was enormous—and it was barrelling right toward them!

Sonia held her breath. She looked at her mother's white face, and watched as she reached up to tidy her hair.

The huge destroyer slowed as it approached them, but their little lifeboat was buffeted by its wake. The boat pitched from side to side. Sonia began to panic. Would they all get dumped into the sea, just when rescue was in sight?

She wrapped her arms around the thwart beside her, preparing for the worst. She felt her mother beside her, tightening her hold on Derek. But then she saw a thick black substance pour out of the side of the destroyer. The liquid spread toward their tiny lifeboat and the water became smooth.

"It's oil," Tommy leaned over to Sonia. "They pour oil on the water to calm it. Standard rescue procedure," he said confidently.

The rescue ship was painted in a zigzag of camouflage markings, *H06* painted in white on the side. Sonia looked up and saw dozens of seamen on the deck, cheering. She felt frozen, like a statue, watching events unfold.

As the waters calmed, the *Marina* crewmen gently rowed to the side of the destroyer. The sailors threw ropes down from the deck and made the lifeboat secure to the side.

Tommy Milligan, her knight in shining armour, was gently peering into her face. "Do you think you can climb up the rope ladder?"

"I think so," she said as bravely as she could. But when she tried to stand, her legs buckled under her and she collapsed onto the bottom of the boat. Tommy gently righted her and sat her back on the thwart.

"You'll need to send down nets for the passengers," Tommy called up to the deck.

Lifeboat crewmen were already scrambling up the rope ladders. A large net was cast down to the lifeboat.

Tommy picked up Derek, "You first, mate," he said, and carefully placed him in a net.

"Thank you ... very much ... sir," Derek said softly as the net was pulled up to the deck. He looks just like a sack of potatoes, thought Sonia.

"You next," said Tommy, sweeping Sonia into his arms and into the net. If it hadn't been for him, she thought, I'd be at the bottom of the ocean.

She was hoisted onto the deck where another sailor helped her out of the net.

"Can you walk?" he asked.

"Yes, of course," she said, but her body swayed and she was lifted up and carried into the ship.

"Hello, miss, I'm Dr. Collison," said a kind voice. "You'll be all right now. We're going to take care of you." The doctor helped Sonia gently remove her soaked and salt-encrusted clothes and guided her into a huge tub of warm water. As she stepped into the tub, the bath water stung her feet as though it was a hundred bees. She cried out. She looked at her feet, so swollen and chaffed that she hardly recognized them. But gradually the salt washed off and the warm water began to relieve and comfort her.

After the bath, she was given a clean sailor's uniform to wear. It was miles too big, but it was dry and comfy. Then one of the sailors carried her to a cot in the officers' mess. Another crewman gave her a mug of warm milk. Sonia could only take tiny sips—her throat was still so raw that every swallow felt like needles slicing into her. But the warm milk soothed her body and she closed her eyes.

* * *

It had taken the destroyer HMS *Hurricane H06*, eighteen hours to get to the disaster site.

They travelled more than three hundred miles, through the storm, pushing the engines to their limit to get there as soon as possible. They arrived at the site of the disaster on

Wednesday, September 18, at 1:00 PM. The SS *City of Benares* had been hit on Tuesday, September 17 at 10:03 PM.

Lieutenant Commander Simms, captain of the *Hurricane*, mapped out a rescue plan based on what he knew about where the *Benares* had gone down. He thought about how far the wind and waves might have moved the lifeboats. He decided to search a twenty-square-mile area starting at a point thirty miles east-northeast from the site where the ship had sunk.

He was looking for twelve lifeboats, and possibly some rafts. He had to be careful. If he went too quickly he could easily miss someone. Or he might swamp a tiny raft as he manoeuvered through the sea.

The captain ordered the sailors out on the deck to scan the sea with binoculars. It was one-thirty in the afternoon when they found the first boat, the one with Sonia and Derek in it.

There were only six hours of daylight left. The captain knew that it was a race against time.

It was two more hours before they saw a second lifeboat.

Chapter Twenty

Ken must have dozed. It was daylight and a light rain was falling. He looked out over the soft grey water. The ocean was eerily quiet. There was nothing of the night's terrors—no other boats, no rafts—nothing to show that the *Benares* had ever been there.

The lascars were taking turns bailing the boat. They only had one pail, and there was always more water coming in, either from the sky or from waves splashing over the sides. The bailing didn't seem to be making much of a difference.

Cadet Critchley and Ramjam Buxoo were stretching a tarpaulin over the bow to create a small covered area.

"You boys might like to have a place out of the rain," said Cadet Critchley. Fred scrunched in and poked his head out to grin at them all.

"This is great! Our own hidey hole," said Fred.

"You look like a duck," said Ken.

"It's a duck hole!" said Howard. "A perfect place to sit out a storm at sea."

"Paul, why don't you come and sit under the tarp with me," said Auntie Mary to one of the other boys. "Give yourself a chance to dry out."

Ken hadn't met Paul on the ship. He was little, probably about seven, Ken figured. He hadn't taken a turn on the Fleming gears last night and he was shaking pretty badly now. Ken watched him hobble into the duck hole with Auntie Mary. He had no shoes on, and it looked like he had a pretty bad cut on his foot.

Mr. Nagorski was sitting straight-backed on the forward thwart. The soft drizzle dripped off his hat. His gloved hands sat still in his lap.

Father O'Sullivan was lying at Mr. Nagorski's feet, on the bottom of the boat. His flu must be getting worse, thought Ken. Derek and another small boy sat on either side of him.

"Where will Peter be?" asked the boy. "He's only five. He's supposed to be on the boat with us. He was in the infirmary last night."

"I'm sure he's fine, Billy," said the priest with effort.

"And Alan?" said Derek. "Mum told me to look after him. And then he got the chicken pox yesterday."

"I'm sure they are both fine. The nurse took them with

her to one of the other boats. They'll be rescued by now and are probably wondering where you are."

Ken watched Steward Purvis investigate the cupboards behind the duck hole, at the bow. Purvis pulled out several barrels and boxes. Ken couldn't see what was in them, but the steward was obviously counting supplies. He wondered how much was there and how long it would have to last. He wondered where their rescue ship was.

The rain started to ease off, and the day began to clear. When the sun was almost directly overhead, Steward Purvis passed around a small beaker of water to each person on the boat. Ken swallowed his greedily. The minute he'd emptied it, he wanted more. He watched as Mr. Nagorski slowly sipped his portion.

"I realize that many of you may still feel thirsty after your water." Officer Cooper stood in the stern, addressing the whole boat. He spoke slowly so that Ramjam could translate his words. Ken heard the words ripple through the lascars in several different languages. When he looked more closely he noticed that the lascars were huddled together in small, but distinct groups.

"You will be tempted, very tempted, to drink the seawater," Cooper continued. "No matter how thirsty you feel, do not, I repeat, *do not under any circumstances drink seawater.*" Ramjam translated the words with a rising voice. The lascars' voices responded in a chatter of unfamiliar sounds.

"If you drink the seawater, you will become disoriented, then you will lose your mind, then you will die. It is as simple as that."

Ken felt guilty for even wanting more water. He looked over at Billy and Derek. Their eyes were wide. He thought they looked a little excited at the idea of someone losing their mind.

After the dipper of water, they were each given a can of condensed milk, a ship's biscuit, and a thin slice of corned beef. Ken realized it was the first food he had had since his last meal on the boat, since his last helping of ice cream. That seemed a very long time ago. He remembered the soft, fluffy breakfast scones. The ship's biscuit was very dry, very hard to swallow. But the milk was a sweet treat.

"I love canned milk!" said Derek delightedly. "My mum gets it for special treats. I can't believe they brought some for us to have on the lifeboat!"

"I never get it at home," said Billy. "Not since the war started. This is great."

The day dragged slowly on with no sight of the rescue boat. Ken wished he had his notebook and pencil, but in all of the confusion, he'd left them behind in the cabin. *I'll have to work extra hard to try and remember everything*, he thought. *I want to be able to draw it all up later. I want to be able to write the story down.*

Ken was beginning to doze off when he overheard Captain Paine from the *Marina* talking in whispers to

Officer Cooper. He was curled up under the wooden side bench in a perfect position to eavesdrop. "Clearly, if there were going to be a rescue it would have come already," he heard Captain Paine say.

"I believe we've drifted out of the area and been missed," the captain continued. "I estimate that we have enough supplies on our boat to last us for eight days. With good winds we can get to Ireland in seven."

"I'm sure that they're still searching for us," said Cooper. "Setting out for Ireland is a terrible risk. I have a woman and six children on board." He breathed in deeply. "I need to wait for rescue."

"Of course you must do what you think best," Paine said. "But I am going to start away, now, while it is still light."

Officer Cooper moved to the middle of the boat, gently displacing the lascars. Ken quietly came out from under the bench and sat up on the bottom of the boat. He saw the *Marina*'s sailors hoisting their sail.

"The *Marina* lifeboat has decided to set sail for Ireland," announced Officer Cooper. "For the time being, we will remain here in the hope of rescue."

"A sound plan, Officer Cooper," said Mr. Nagorski.

"Ireland?" said Auntie Mary. "How long would that take?"

"The *Marina* lifeboat should be able to make it in six or seven days," answered Officer Cooper. "Our boat is heavier, and would take longer. In my judgment, we are better to wait here for rescue."

The smaller lifeboat's sails filled with the wind. Her sailors waved goodbye. "Best of luck, little sailors!" they called out. Ken and Fred stood up carefully and saluted. Imagine, sailing all the way to Ireland. Imagine being at sea for seven days! He wished he could go with them, instead of sitting here doing nothing, waiting to be rescued.

The winds were strong. It wasn't long before the *Marina's* lifeboat was out of sight. They were alone. A deep quiet settled into lifeboat 12.

Officer Cooper called to Ken. "What's your name, son?"

"Kenneth James Sparks, sir," said Ken in what he hoped was his best naval voice.

"Have you got good eyesight, Master Sparks?"

"Excellent, sir."

"Right then, you'll take the first lookout. You're to sit in the bow and keep your eyes open. The rescue ship may be a long way off and they may not see us. Your job is to see them. Then our job will be to get their attention."

"Aye, aye, sir," said Ken.

Officer Cooper turned to Signalman Mayhew.

"What we need is some kind of a flag, something that can be seen from a distance."

"I can't find anything of the sort on board, sir," replied Mayhew. "I've searched the stores and there are no flags or fabrics of any kind."

"I have something you can use." Auntie Mary called out

loudly from the duck hole. She disappeared under the tarp. A moment later, Ken saw her arm emerge, flourishing a pink petticoat.

Mayhew and Cooper looked at each other, embarrassed. "Come on," called Auntie Mary from her spot, "take it. It won't bite and you need something to put on the mast."

Ramjam carefully worked his way to the duck hole, stepping around and between the other lascars. He bowed respectfully to Auntie Mary and took the petticoat. He carried it reverently to Officer Cooper. In no time, Mayhew had shinnied up the mast and tied it onto the top. They had their flag. A pink flag.

The swell was strong, and the boat pitched in the gale. Ken sat perched in the bow, scouring the horizon for any sign of movement.

The afternoon wore on. The sun peeked through the clouds. There was still no sign of a rescue ship. Ken was relieved of his lookout duties, replaced by Cadet Critchley.

The excitement of being shipwrecked was wearing off a bit, and Ken couldn't help feeling just a bit bored.

Suddenly, Gunner Peard stood up on the starboard side of the boat. He stripped off his clothes down to his underwear, stepped on the side bench, and dove into the water with a splash.

"What's he doing?!" Billy screamed, in a panic.

Peard's grizzled head popped above the surface on the port side of the boat. He laughed and shook water from his hair. He started singing as he swam a backstroke, keeping alongside the boat.

> We'll rant and we'll roar like true British sailors,
> We'll rant and we'll roar all on the salt seas.
> Until we strike soundings in the channel of old
> England;
> From Ushant to Scilly is thirty-five leagues.

Peard sang out lustily.

Ken laughed and clapped. This was a great show.

"Hurray for Harry the Gunner!" cried Howard.

"Has he no sense of decency?" Auntie Mary hissed to Father O'Sullivan.

"Come on in, lads! Nothing to be frightened of," Peard called out.

Ken watched Peard doing a lazy backstroke around the lifeboat. It looked so easy.

> Now let ev'ry man drink off his full bumper,
> And let ev'ry man drink off his full glass;
> We'll drink and be jolly and drown melancholy,
> And here's to the health of each true-hearted lass.

"Don't listen to that man," said Auntie Mary. She had

come out of the duck hole and was glaring at Peard.

"She's right, boys," said Father O'Sullivan weakly. "You stay here in the boat."

"Suit yourself, lads," said the gunner, as he squirted water between his teeth. He grabbed the gunwales to hoist himself back into the boat.

"Come join me over here in the duck hole, boys," said Auntie Mary. "Come tell me what you remember about being on the *Benares*."

Reluctantly, Ken worked his way into the duck hole to sit with the others. *I'm not a great swimmer anyway*, he thought.

"Come on," said Auntie Mary cheerfully. "Squish in. There's room for everyone. Now tell me, what do you remember?"

"I remember the waiters' uniforms," said little Paul. "White and blue."

"I remember Miss Grierson and the moving picture she was making," said Fred. "I can't wait to see how it turns out!"

"I remember the food," said Howard.

"The ice cream!" said Derek.

"Miss?" Fred said. "Which would you rather be? Bombed in London or torpedoed in the Atlantic?"

"Yes, miss, which would you rather be? Bombed in London or torpedoed in the Atlantic?" repeated Billy.

"Well," said Auntie Mary as she began to massage Paul's feet distractedly, "I'm not sure I really like either. But I would have to say that this is a pretty big adventure."

Ken thought about the bomb shelters. He remembered the noise of the bombs, the shaking of the bricks in the archway above him in Wembley. He thought of dirt filling his mouth, bricks smashing his skull.

He looked out over the expanse of the ocean. He knew which he thought was better.

A long day passed. As the sun began to set, Officer Cooper called for everyone's attention.

"We have now been on this lifeboat for eighteen hours. I have to assume that all of the other boats have now been found and rescued."

Ken saw Auntie Mary look over at Father O'Sullivan, who was propped up in the bottom of the boat. *This is not good news*, he thought.

"I have re-assessed our situation and it is my belief that the rescue ship has unfortunately missed us," continued Officer Cooper. "Therefore, our only option is to head for Ireland."

Ken heard Auntie Mary gasp.

"Ireland?" said Father O'Sullivan, coughing.

"This is madness," said Mr. Nagorski. He'd been silent most of the day, but his voice was now strong, and angry. "Officer Cooper. Surely it is better to stay here, where we have a hope of being found by a rescue vessel. I can't believe that the *Winchelsea* has just gone off and left us. Surely, the destroyer will be back looking for us. If we leave the area they will have no idea of where to look."

"I repeat, Mr. Nagorski, every indication shows that a rescue vessel has missed us. It is accepted naval practice in such a situation for a shipwrecked crew to make for the nearest land. What is more, by heading for land we have a much better chance of coming across another boat—a shipping vessel, warship, even a fishing boat. As captain of this lifeboat, this is my decision. We will set sail in the morning."

Ramjam translated Officer Cooper's decision for the lascars. They looked confused and called out to Ramjam. He raised his hands and spoke again. At his words, all were quiet.

There was a deep silence on the boat. Eventually, Auntie Mary asked Ramjam what he had said to calm the crew.

"Allah the compassionate will save us, if He so wishes. Or he will send storms if He thinks it best. God is wise."

Ken hoped there would be no more storms. He wondered if Allah had given them enough food and water to get them to Ireland.

Chapter Twenty-One

The sky changed colour. The sun was starting to set. Bess's nose was filled with salt. It was getting hard to breathe.

She knew she had to keep going for Beth. But it was going to be hard, very hard to face another night.

"Beth ... one ... more night ..." Her voice was barely a whisper. She heard Beth trying to speak and turned her head to look at her. And then she looked past Beth and saw...

"A ship," she said.

"No ... imagin ... ation ..." whispered Beth.

But Bess could see it. A huge destroyer, painted in zigzags. It looked very real.

She couldn't call. Her voice didn't work. She couldn't wave. Her arms didn't work. Would anyone see them?

The destroyer wasn't moving. It was just sitting there. Maybe it was a ghost ship after all.

Then, through blurred vision she saw something else. It looked like a small boat coming closer. Toward them. There were men rowing. She heard words, but couldn't understand them. Maybe she was dreaming again. Or maybe ... *they're Germans*, she thought.

We've got to fight them.

Not sure I can.

Loud cheering.

A rugby match?

"Come on, me darlings!" A voice cut through her dream. "We are going to get you off of there." *They don't sound like Germans*, thought Bess.

Everything went black.

When Bess woke up she was in a large, cushioned chair. She looked slowly around. There were sailors everywhere, staring at her. She saw Beth on a sofa at the other side of the small room. She blinked.

"Miss?" said one of the sailors softly. "Would you like a bit of hot soup?" He tenderly handed her a steaming mug. As she raised her hands, she saw two bloated, jelly like objects, with bits of skin hanging off them.

"I ... I don't think I can hold anything," she whispered.

The sailor held the cup to her lips. But she couldn't

make her throat swallow the thick liquid. She shook her head.

Just then, an officer came into the room. He knelt down beside her.

"Hello. I'm Officer Collinson, the medic on the ship," he said gently. "Can you tell me your name?"

"Bess. Bess Walder."

"How are you feeling, Bess?"

"A bit dizzy."

"Bess, I'd like you to try to drink just a bit of this warm sugar water. It's got a bit of rum in it to help you sleep a bit. You've had quite a shock," Dr. Collinson added.

"Is Beth all right?" Bess asked.

"Your friend? She feels about the same as you."

Bess took a sip of the drink that Dr. Collinson offered her. It slid down her parched throat. She took another sip and closed her eyes. She opened them again. The sailor with the cup of soup was looking at her.

"Did you ... rescue me?" Bess asked slowly.

"Yes, miss." She saw that his eyes were filled with tears.

"What ... what is your name?" Bess's eyes were starting to close.

"Albert Gorman, miss. You just sleep now," he said softly.

Bess began to drift off. "Thank you very much, Mr. Gorman," she murmured as her eyes closed.

Sonia was bundled in blankets, hanging snugly in a hammock in the officer's mess. She felt the ship's engines stop and start up again. Stop and start. Stop and start. After each time, sailors brought in more rescued passengers from the *Benares*.

From her hammock, Sonia watched her mother help Dr. Collinson tend to survivors as they were brought in. Waterlogged people came in for cups of hot soup and tots of rum before being tucked into hammocks, cots, and bunks throughout the ship. Broken bits of stories came to her ears.

"... five of us on a raft ..."

"... swimming until someone plucked me out ..."

"... there were thirty-one ..."

With every new arrival, Sonia's mother asked, "Have you seen a girl called Barbara Bech? Have you seen my daughter?"

Then Sonia heard singing, a solo voice, high, like the choirboy she heard at Christmas. She wondered if she was dreaming.

> Rule Britannia,
> Britannia rule the waves
> Britons never, never, never
> Shall be slaves!

She opened her eyes and saw a sailor walking in with a bright red sack slung over his shoulder. Christmas? The sack was singing.

The sailor set the sack down. "I think you can take this off now," he said. "It's done the job."

"I promised my mother I'd keep it on until I got off the boat in Canada."

"Colin!" Sonia shrieked.

"Well, you'll not be heading to Canada now," said the sailor. "I think she won't mind, seein' how you're safe under the protection of the Royal Navy."

Just then another sailor came in, carrying a girl, wrapped in a blanket. He walked over to Sonia's mother.

"Now just look what I found all wrapped up safe in bed beside the ship's funnel," he beamed.

"Barbara!" Sonia's mother burst into tears.

* * *

The sun set.

Lieutenant Commander Simms had done all he could. He had found twelve lifeboats, some overturned, some empty, some filled with lifeless bodies. He'd found one lifeboat from the *Marina*, with a crew who had picked up some passengers and lascars from the *Benares*. He'd found two girls, barely alive, clinging onto the overturned hull of a lifeboat. He'd searched every inch of his 20-mile box search.

That's it, he thought, with a deep melancholy. Of the 408 passengers and crew, he had rescued only 106. Some of the children were in pretty bad shape. He wasn't sure if they'd survive.

There were no more survivors to look for. It was dark. There was nothing more he could do.

He set sail for Scotland.

He didn't know about lifeboat 12.

PART III

Chapter Twenty-Two

Bess's eyes opened. Her brain took time to catch up. She was surprised to find herself in a comfortable bed, wearing no clothes. Her wet nightdress and green dressing gown were gone. She felt around on a table beside the bed, and found her glasses. Someone had cleaned them. How on earth had they stayed on? She carefully put them on over her salt-scarred face.

A large tub of water was sitting in the middle of the room.

"I could do without seeing water again," she said aloud.

"Me too," said a familiar voice from across the room.

"Beth!"

Beth gave a weak wave from the sofa on the other side of the room.

Just then, Dr. Collison came in.

"Glad to see you two awake," he said cheerfully.

"Where are we?" said Bess.

"You're in the captain's quarters. You've been given VIP treatment. Best beds on the ship, by all accounts. How are you feeling?"

"Tired," said Beth.

"Pretty dizzy," offered Bess. Truth be told, she felt horrible. Worse than the worst flu she'd ever had. She was shaking and sweating, with pains running up and down her body.

But she was alive. She was no longer in the ocean.

"You need to get into the bath. You've got to get that salt washed off your body. And you need to get some fresh water into your system," said the doctor.

"I'm not sure I can ..."

"You must. Doctor's orders," he smiled kindly.

He carefully helped her into the tub. The water stung where her skin had been scraped raw.

Suddenly her eyes welled with tears.

"How am I going to tell them?" she wept. "How can I tell my parents that I lost Louis? He didn't even want to come on the trip. It was all my idea. And now he's gone. They will never, ever forgive me ..." Tears streamed down her face.

Dr. Collison knelt down beside Bess.

"You mustn't think of it that way," he said quietly. "They'll be so happy to have you home safely. So grateful to have you." He paused. "Some mummies and daddies won't have anyone coming home."

Bess sobbed. It was an unspeakable thought, and he had said it. She felt guilty for crying. But she felt swallowed up by sorrow.

The reality of this war was more horrific than anyone could have possibly imagined.

Dr. Collinson looked in on Bess and Beth every few hours throughout the night. He changed the bandages on their feet and wiped their cuts carefully with purple iodine. He gave them tablets to help to bring their fever down and to dull the pain. He brought clean sailor's shirts for them to wear and told them they were confined to bed.

Bess hurt everywhere. She felt bruised in every part of her body. But mostly she was sick at heart. She ached for her brother. Beth tried to make her feel better, reminding her of what Dr. Collinson had said and of how happy her parents would be to have her come home. But she couldn't help feeling guilty. The trip had been her idea. She had pushed for it. She had persuaded her parents and Louis. It was her fault.

Suddenly there was a loud knock at the door.

"Come in?" said Beth. Bess turned her back to the door.

"Miss Walder?" said a commanding voice. "Sit up, young lady." Bess thought she'd never felt less like sitting up. She turned her head slowly to see the ship's captain standing in the doorway, looking very stern. *Perhaps he wants us out of his bedroom*, she thought.

"I have something you lost," he said. And with that he reached around behind him and brought forward a small boy in an oversized sailor's uniform and cap down to his ears.

"What are you doing lying in bed?" the boy asked, grinning. "Get up."

"LOUIS!" screamed Bess and he bounded across the room and into her arms.

"We were thrown out of the lifeboat before we even got to the water." Louis was sitting at the end of Bess's bed, eating through a mound of chocolate biscuits that neither Bess nor Beth could swallow.

"The water was so cold, and I kept going under. I tried to remember what Dad had shown us, but the waves just kept pushing me down. I was sure I was a goner."

Bess could hardly listen to Louis' words. She just wanted to stare at him, to drink him in.

"The life jacket saved me. I kept popping up to the surface. And I kept moving. Kicking like crazy.

"Suddenly someone grabbed me. It was Michael, swimming in the water. He's a terrific swimmer! He pulled me over to the boat and Mr. Proudfoot—he told me he was the bartender at the other end of the ship—he lifted me in.

"There was a lot of water in the boat. It was almost up

to my waist. Michael was still in the water, swimming, and he got more boys in. There were lots of us there. I was really glad to see Rex. He was worried about his little sister Marion, though. He couldn't find her when we were getting on the lifeboat.

"And then they gave us some rum! It burned and made me cough, but it made me feel a little warmer. Michael was in the boat then and he had some too. I guess there was no one left for him to save.

"After he had the rum, he looked pretty tired. Mr. Proudfoot said he'd tired himself out, saving so many of us.

"I must have fallen asleep, because when I woke up he wasn't there anymore. Neither were some of the other kids. But Mr. Proudfoot and another man, they looked after me. They tried to hold me and Rex out of the water. Mr. Proudfoot is really tall, and he tucked me under his arm to keep me a bit dry until the rescue boat came.

"When I woke up this morning I was feeling a lot better, so one of the sailors showed me around the ship. Then I saw your old green dressing gown hanging up to dry in the boiler room, so I knew you were around somewhere. And the captain brought me here."

Bess tried to make sense of what Louis said. Michael Rennie, the strong, handsome escort—he died? How had she survived and he hadn't? It was all too much, too impossibly painful. She looked at Beth. She saw tears streaming down her face.

"Bessie?"

"Yes, Louis?"

"I don't want to go to Canada anymore."

"Neither do I," she reassured him. "It's all right. The ship is taking us home."

"Bessie?"

"Yes, Louis?"

"I lost my engine."

"I know."

"But the rest of the train is still at home, right?"

"Yes. The rest of the train is safe at home, waiting for you."

* * *

Sonia was sitting with Derek, Barbara, and Colin, having sweet tea in the officers' mess. Her mother was talking to Mr. Davis, the man from the BBC.

"I can't thank you enough for what you did for us. We wouldn't be alive, had it not been for you," she said.

There were a couple of other children in the mess, but Sonia didn't recognize them. They must be the seavacuees, she thought. There weren't very many. Sonia counted five. She heard that there were a couple of girls in really bad shape sleeping in the captain's quarters. Perhaps another ship had picked up the rest of the children.

News that they were heading to Scotland spread quickly

through the ship. It would take two days to reach the port at Greenock.

"I never wanted to leave in the first place," said a woman who Sonia recognized from the lounge of the *Benares*. "And I certainly won't be doing *this* again."

Sonia had to admit that she was very happy to be going back home. She thought she could face any number of bombs after what they'd been through.

The next morning, Sonia went with her mother to a ritual burial at sea. Three boys who had been pulled out of the water the day before had died in the night. "Some of the seavacuees," said Sonia's mother. Rescue had come just hours too late.

"All hands bury the dead." The call went through the ship. They went to the quarterdeck and joined the crew and other passengers who were well enough to walk.

Colin sat quietly beside Sonia. The captain had slowed the ship so that it was barely moving. The crew all stood at attention.

There were Union Jacks lying on top of each of the three cloth-covered bodies.

"You have all been through a terrible trial," said Lieutenant Commander Simms to everyone, "but you have survived. Three hundred and six souls perished when the *Benares* went down. These three little boys represent them all. This burial at sea is to honour all of those who are not returning."

The ship's chaplain read the Lord's Prayer. Three times he said, "And we therefore commit his body to the deep. May God rest his soul."

The ship's massive six-inch gun fired three times. A young sailor played "Taps" on the bugle.

Sonia leaned against her mother. The crew saluted as each small body gently slid down a ramp and floated away.

Chapter Twenty-Three

The sound of moaning woke Ken up. He'd been dreaming that his legs were pinned under a truck. He couldn't move them at all. They were cold and stiff and hurt so much. He realized it was the sound of his own moaning that woke him.

He opened his eyes. He was squeezed in beside Howard and Fred on the wooden bottom of the boat. He tried to stretch his legs, but he banged into Father O'Sullivan, who was flat on his back in the middle of the boat. Ken kicked his legs up in the air, and shook them to try and get the numbness out.

With the morning, there was a bit of sunshine, and his face felt dry and warm. A lot of rain had fallen in the night, and there was water sloshing about in the boat. *Which was why my back is sopping*, thought Ken.

We'll have a lot of bailing to do today.

But the bailing bucket had other uses first. There were no toilets on the lifeboat. Gunner Peard had shown the boys how to pee off the side of the boat. "There's a trick to standing so you don't fall out of the boat," he'd said, showing them how to push their hips forward and their shoulders backward. They'd almost fallen out of the boat just from laughing so hard.

For other business, they had to ask to use the bucket. But with so little to eat they didn't need to use it very often.

It was different for Auntie Mary, though. She was allowed to use the bucket whenever she needed. "Memsahib needs the bucket," Ramjam would call out, and it was passed down to her in the duck hole. Ken, Fred, and Howard would stand as best they could with their backs to the duck hole to give her some privacy.

The other morning ritual was the lascars' prayers. Ken began to recognize that there were three distinct groups, each wearing their own kind of turban or cap and saying different kinds of prayers. Some sat on their feet and bowed their heads, like Father O'Sullivan. Others squatted, facing east—which was the direction that the sun came up—and bent their bodies down to touch their foreheads to the bottom of the boat. Others lay completely face downwards. That meant everyone else had to shift positions. Yesterday, they'd said prayers several times during the day. This morning, they started just as the sun was coming up.

Before they said their prayers, the lascars rinsed their mouths out with seawater. Ken tried to imagine rinsing his mouth and not swallowing. He wasn't sure he could do it. He was so very thirsty. They all waited until the lascars had finished their prayers before Steward Purvis passed out the breakfast rations.

A beaker of water, a ship's biscuit, half a sardine. Forty-six dips of water, forty-six biscuits, forty-six half sardines.

"Bless us, O Lord, and these, Thy gifts, which we are about to receive from Thy bounty. Through Christ, our Lord. Amen." Father O'Sullivan crossed himself weakly from the bottom of the boat.

Saying grace seemed to make the meal last a bit longer.

Ken remembered to drink his water slowly this time. The water dipper was tiny. There were probably only three little sips in total.

"I'm still thirsty," Paul complained softly.

"What?" Gunner Peard was standing in the bow, near the duck hole, stretching. "What did you say?" he asked Paul.

"I'm still thirsty," Paul repeated. Ken saw a slight look of panic in his eyes.

"Have you no buttons?" asked Gunner Peard.

"Buttons?"

"Yeah," growled Peard, "Buttons. Everybody knows that if you're thirsty you have to suck on your buttons. Didn't that school marm teach you anything?"

Auntie Mary glared at Gunner Peard, but said nothing.

Ken watched Paul and Billy shyly put their pyjama buttons in their mouths. When he was sure no one was looking, he put one in his mouth. It just tasted salty, like everything else on the boat.

"I'm going to use my lucky lamb," said Derek. "The one the Reverend King gave me back on the boat. Maybe it will taste like a roast."

Suddenly, the boat rocked. Splash! Harry the Gunner was swimming in vigorous circles around the boat. "Mr. Peard," called Ken, "Why do you keep swimming every morning?"

"Got to keep in practice in case we get torpedoed again!"

Ken burst out laughing at the thought of their little lifeboat being torpedoed. Looked like they couldn't even be found, let alone torpedoed. Peard sang as he swam.

> Run rabbit—run rabbit—Run! Run! Run!
> Run rabbit —run rabbit—Run! Run! Run!
> Bang! Bang! Bang! Bang!

Ken and Howard joined in. "Bang! Bang! Bang! Bang!" The Germans had torpedoed their ship, but the Royal Navy would rescue them and blow that U-boat out of the water.

When Peard got back in the boat, Cadet Critchley and Officer Cooper ran up the sail.

"Ireland, next stop!" said Officer Cooper. "Master Ken Sparks, Master Howard Claytor: you're on duty at the

Fleming gears. With your muscles, we'll get there all the sooner."

Ken and Howard pushed and pulled along with Critchley and Purvis. There was a good wind. They seemed to be moving at a good clip, but with no shore and nothing stationary, it was impossible to tell how fast they were going.

By the time Fred and Derek took their shift on the gears, Ken's hands were blistered and sore. Not that he was going to complain. He realized that being a sailor was hard work. He knew his blisters would turn to calluses and his hands would get tougher and stronger. He sat on the side bench, looking over the endless sea. He dipped his hands in the salty water. It stung, but the pain made him feel more grown-up. The day wore on with no sign of land or rescue.

"I know," said Auntie Mary. "How about a game of I Spy? I spy with my little eye, something that is pink," she said.

"The flag," said Fred. "There's nothing else pink anywhere."

"Good," she said. "Now it's your turn."

"I spy with my little eye something that is blue," said Fred.

"Water," said Howard. "This is boring. There isn't exactly a lot to see."

Ken's legs were cramping terribly. He wanted to find a place to sit by himself, where he could stretch, but it was impossible. Howard was on one side of him, little Billy squirming on the other. Auntie Mary was in the duck hole with Paul. There was a little bit of room there, if he wanted to squish in and lie down. But he'd be pretty cramped.

He thought about going over to the other side of the boat. Maybe Mr. Nagorski could slide over, just a little bit. But Gunner Peard was there, cleaning his nails with a penknife, and he sure didn't want to disturb him. Besides, to even get to the other side, he'd have to step over Father O'Sullivan. Further down, in the middle of the boat, the lascars were spread around the Fleming gears in their groups. They hummed to themselves, occasionally speaking a few words that sounded like a prayer of some kind. Officer Cooper stood in the stern at the tiller. No one could move and there was nothing to do.

"What about Animal, Vegetable, Mineral?" offered Auntie Mary. "Why don't you start, Paul?"

Ken looked over at Paul. He looked like he was in a kind of trance. His face was blank, and his salt-encrusted mouth hung loosely. His eyes were open, but he didn't look like he was seeing anything.

Fear suddenly flashed through Ken. His mind was flooded with images of people in the water, screaming. What had happened to Terry? Or that boy Louis, with his train engine? Did they get rescued? What had happened to Captain Nicoll? Had he actually gone down with the ship, the way that captains are supposed to do? The reality of the situation started to flood through him. People have died, he realized with a shock.

And what about us? Ireland is a long way away. What if our water runs out? You need water to live, thought Ken.

He remembered a plant that his stepmother had forgotten to water. He had noticed it one day, on a hot windowsill. It was all thin and grey. The leaves had fallen off. Would it be like that for them? He looked at Paul's face again. It looked colourless and withered already.

Will we dry out and die here in the ocean?

Ken shivered as this last thought took hold of him. As if in response to his thoughts, Auntie Mary suddenly said, "All right, gather around me. It's time for a story."

"A story? What kind of story?" asked Billy.

"Is it an adventure? Will there be pirates?" asked Howard.

Suddenly, everyone was awake. Even Paul's face lit up.

"It's a Bulldog Drummond story," she said.

Bulldog Drummond! The best! The bravest of the brave. A hero's hero. Bulldog Drummond, hero of the Great War, who came home to find life after the war dull. Ken had memorized the best part.

Bulldog Drummond put an ad in a local paper:

> *Demobilized officer finding peace incredibly tedious would welcome diversion. Legitimate if possible; but crime of a humorous description, no objection. Excitement essential.*

"The Contessa de Guy," began Auntie Mary, "had assembled some of the richest and most dastardly men in the whole world in a remote corner of Africa. In Morocco, in fact. Of course, her name wasn't really Contessa de Guy, for she was none other than the conniving and vicious Irma, arch enemy of Bulldog Drummond."

Ken saw that even the lascars were all listening and watching Auntie Mary, although he was sure they couldn't understand a word. But they could see that she was telling an exciting story. Even Mr. Nagorski and Harry the Gunner were listening.

"Irma, distraught over the fact that Drummond had killed her lover Carl Peterson. So she concocted a scheme that would ruin Drummond, cause the collapse of the manufacturing industry, and ultimately bankrupt England.

"Irma wouldn't rest until she destroyed everything that an Englishman holds dear. She set the wheels in motion for her grand plans."

She stopped.

"What's next, Auntie Mary?" asked Derek.

"You'll have to wait until storytime tomorrow," she said.

"No!" cried Ken. There were groans all around.

"I'm sorry," she said, "but that's all there is for today. *Bulldog Drummond and the Tale of the African Diamonds*, to be continued tomorrow."

Ken looked out at the endless sea. For a brief time Auntie Mary's story had made him forget where he was. He had even forgotten his thirst. To be continued tomorrow. It seemed impossible to imagine that they would be sitting here tomorrow. But if they were heading to Ireland, they might be here for many more days.

At least he could look forward to Bulldog Drummond.

The wind picked up as the sun began to set on their second night in the lifeboat. "Looks like we're heading into a bit of weather," said Officer Cooper. "Purvis, Critchley, get that sail down. Peard, put the sea anchor out."

Ken lay scrunched on the bottom of the boat with Derek, Billy, Fred, and Howard, covered by a blanket. Paul was beside Auntie Mary, covered by the only other blanket in the boat.

As it became windy and the sky grew dark, Ken looked out over the gloomy boat. The lascars were piled in their groups, curled on top of each other. They looked so cold with no blankets, no shelter.

The boat began to pitch and roll. Ken's legs felt so cramped that he didn't know how he would ever be able to sleep. He hadn't walked in two days. Shooting pains tightened the muscles along the sides of his shins. He kicked out, trying to stretch them, and banged into Billy in the dark.

"Watch it," said Billy, but his voice sounded funny. Ken realized that he was crying. And as Billy's sobs grew louder, Ken heard Derek start to cry too.

"I'm worried about Alan. He doesn't know where I am," sobbed Derek.

"Peter needs me," cried Billy.

"Hey now, what's all this?" Gunner Peard growled from

his perch on the gunwale beside them. He poked his head into the duck hole.

"What's this sniffing and snivelling? It's just a little shipwreck. No big thing at all. You just wait. Another day or two and we'll be rescued. Do you think the Royal Navy is going to let you down? Brave boys need feel no fear."

"But Alan ..." Derek started.

"Your brothers are feastin' on cake and ice cream. Havin' a great party. But they'll be sorry to have missed this! It's not every boy who gets to spend time on a lifeboat! Now you close your eyes and get off to sleep. We'll need your muscles in the morning to push those Fleming gears."

Derek and Billy were quiet and Ken was just starting to nod off to sleep when he overheard Peard talking to Mr. Nagorski. What he heard sent a stab of fear through his body.

"We ought to be halfway to Ireland by now," the gunner hissed to Mr. Nagorski. "Cooper isn't working those lascars half hard enough. They need to put their backs into those damned Fleming gears. Our supplies aren't going to last forever. In fact, I'd be surprised if we make it through another day, two at most. The chances of making it out of here alive are slim."

"Mr. Peard," Mr. Nagorski said, "I would appreciate it if you kept your calculations to yourself. While I may share some of your concerns, I don't think it a good idea to further demoralize the boat."

Peard sniffed. "Have it your own way. Just don't say I didn't warn you."

Ken felt Derek's body jerk with sobs. Before he could stop himself, he began to cry too.

"Now, now," said Auntie Mary softly. "There's no room for tears here. You are all heroes of a real adventure. Have you ever heard of a hero who snivelled? Why, any boy in England would love to take your place in this lifeboat right now," she said. "When you get home, they'll write stories about you."

Ken was ashamed of his tears. He imagined being the star of an adventure book. He looked at Derek. Derek looked back with a small smile. Derek Drummond. Bulldog Ken.

Who ever heard of a hero who snivelled?

Chapter Twenty-Four

"Bessie, there's a whole crowd of people waiting! I can see photographers and reporters and ... oh! There's Mr. Shakespeare, from Liverpool." Louis couldn't wait to tell everyone about how he almost drowned.

It was exactly a week since they'd left Liverpool harbour on the *City of Benares*. Instead of Canada, they were arriving in Scotland on the HMS *Hurricane*.

Bess and Beth were both still too weak to walk. They were carried from the ship on stretchers. Louis was practically dancing by Bess's side. As they were leaving the ship, Bess asked her stretcher-bearer to stop. She beckoned to Albert Gorman who was standing on the deck watching all of the passengers leave. He bent down to her.

"Thank you again," she said. "I would have died." She gave him a soft kiss on his rough cheek.

Mr. Shakespeare was on the dock, yelling at the reporters. "No photographs of the CORB children! And no published stories until we've alerted next of kin. This directive comes from the prime minister himself. Understood?"

Bess, Beth, and Louis were brought down the gangplank with the four other children from the CORB program. There was little Johnny who kept getting lost and who had such a hard time keeping hold of his life jacket. Bess had heard that Johnny's brother Bobby had given him his own life jacket when they boarded their lifeboat. There was Jack, Joyce's brother; and Rex, Marion's brother. Bess hoped that Marion and Joyce had stayed together. Joyce. She'd never forget the feeling of her hand. But she couldn't think about that now.

She was slowly carried forward with Johnny, Jack, Rex and Eleanor following behind. Eleanor had been in the lifeboat with Miss Day and stewardess Annie Ryan. Patricia had been there too, apparently, except she hadn't made it through. Eleanor was having a hard time walking and was leaning on Miss Ryan. Louis told her that Eleanor hadn't spoken a word since she'd been rescued.

Mr. Shakespeare stood stiffly at the bottom of the gangplank, looking as though he hadn't slept in days. He stared from one to the next and turned to Lieutenant Commander Simms.

"Is this ... all? Seven?" He looked down, then back up at the captain. "There were ninety," he said softly.

Bess's stretcher-bearers started to move forward, but Mr. Shakespeare held them back. "If I may. Just one moment," he said, turning to Bess. "I need to get everyone's name," he cleared his throat. "I have to send telegrams."

"I'm Bess. Bess Walder. This is my brother Louis," She reached out to Beth in the stretcher beside her. "And this is my best friend Beth Cummings. Will you let our mothers know that we are home in England?"

"We are going to take care of you at the Smithson Hospital. I'll let your parents know where to find you." He looked down at Louis. "Are you going to come with the other children to the hotel in Glasgow? The Lord Provost is putting you up, for as long as you need, until your parents can come and get you."

"I'd rather stay with Bessie, if it's all right, sir. None of my friends from the ship are there, so I'd just as soon be with Bessie and Beth."

"Mr. Shakespeare?" Bess called out, as the stretcher-bearer lifted her up. "Can you also tell our parents that we'd rather not be a part of the CORB program anymore? We'd rather stay here, in England. Even with the bombs."

Mr. Shakespeare looked deeply into Bess's eyes. "It's all right, Miss Walder. There is no more CORB program. The government will not be sending any children overseas anymore." Bess heard him choke back a sob. "I'm so terribly sorry."

* * *

Sonia stood at the top of the gangplank with her mother, Barbara, Derek, and Colin. It was not the glamorous arrival in Canada that she had imagined. She was wearing her ruined camel-hair coat over the torn outfit she had put on in her cabin three nights ago. Although her mother had tried to comb her hair, she knew that she looked a fright.

A crowd of reporters were gathered at the bottom of the gangplank and there were flash bulbs going off everywhere.

"Can't they wait until we've got some clean clothes on before taking photographs?" Sonia's mother was horrified.

"I think I can help the situation," said Mr. Davis. As he headed down the gangplank, he called down in a loud voice, "Hello boys! Eric Davis from the BBC. Have I got a story for you!"

The reporters and photographers swarmed over to Mr. Davis while Sonia's mother steered them in the other direction.

"First thing I am going to do is to go to the shops and get us all clean clothes," she said. "You too, Colin. You can't walk around Scotland in your pyjamas!"

* * *

Bess and Beth were in side-by-side beds in a private room in the hospital. They were treated like royalty by the hospital staff. They were black and blue from head to toe and the shape and colour of their bruises fascinated the hospital doctor. He brought all of the nurses to see them. A reporter had come in and insisted on asking her questions. But Bess really just wanted to sleep.

When a stocky woman with bright dark eyes came into the room several days later, Bess knew her immediately as Beth's mother. She held Beth and didn't say anything for a very long time. Then she turned to Bess.

"Hello, Bess. I have already read so much about you in the paper. I understand your mother is coming up from London?"

"Yes. She should be here in a few days."

"I think I have you to thank for my daughter's survival."

"No, Mrs. Cummings, not at all. We looked after each other. I couldn't have made it without Beth."

Mrs. Cummings looked at her daughter. "I've spoken to the doctor. He says that as long as we have a nurse come in to bandage your feet every day, there's no reason why I can't take you home. The hospital is going to give us a wheelchair, since you are not allowed to walk yet." She sighed. "I'm just so glad that I can take you home."

Bess knew that Beth had been worried about her mother. "It was the thought of her that kept me alive that night," she had said to Bess. She knew how important it was for them to be together again. But it was going to be hard to say goodbye.

"You'll write to me?" said Beth, reading her mind.

"Every day," said Bess. "And as soon as the war is over, I'm coming to Liverpool. I want to meet those brothers of yours!"

Beth smiled weakly and reached up for her mother's hand. Mrs. Cummings turned to Bess.

"You're family now," she said. "You stay with us as long as you can. I'd take you with me now, except I expect your parents probably want to have some time with you first."

Bess smiled. "Yes. Louis and I are pretty excited to be going home."

Mrs. Cummings settled her daughter into the wheelchair.

"Beth?" Bess called to her. Beth wheeled herself close to Bess's bed. "Thank you," Bess said quietly, hugging her hard.

"Thank you, dear Queen Bess."

Bess laughed. "Goodbye, dear Princess Elizabeth."

After Beth left, Bess missed her mother and father more than ever. She was impatient to go home.

"Your mum's been slowed up by the Germans," said her nurse. "I heard on the radio this mornin' that London's takin' it pretty hard. Those jerries have been bombin' the train tracks, so they have to keep reroutin' the trains."

"Oh," said Bess with a gasp.

"Now, don't you go worryin'," continued the nurse. "Your mum'll be fine. She's just got to be taking the long 'way round, is all. Could take the better part of the week to get up here to Scotland. Best you just rest up now."

Bess was happy to spend most of the time sleeping. She was more tired than she imagined it was possible to be. But she was worried about Louis, afraid he might get into mischief wandering around the hospital.

"Louis, are you sure you don't want to go to the hotel with the others? I really don't want you to get into trouble here."

Louis laughed. "I don't think the nurses would let me go. They are having too much fun playing cards in the nurses' station."

"What?"

"I taught them how to play Happy Families! Now they can't get enough of it," said Louis. "But it's all right, Bessie. I make sure they still get their work done."

At this Bess laughed and decided not to worry any more. Aside from the card games, she knew that Louis also had many new toys to play with. Ever since an article about them had come out in the paper, people had been coming to see them. They always brought gifts. Louis was thrilled with his brand-new Hornby train set.

When Bess's mother finally walked into the hospital room, Bess was horrified.

"Oh, Mummy! You look awful! You look like you've walked from one end of the country to the other!"

"I practically have," she said, scooping Bess into an enormous hug.

Bess felt a wave of emotion begin to wash over her. She knew that if she started to cry, she might never stop. It was the thought of her mother that had kept her alive and now here she was, finally, warm and familiar. Except—

"What are you wearing? That's not your dress!" Bess spoke the words without thinking, just to say something to stop the wave. Through the entire ordeal, she'd pictured her mother just the way she looked when she'd left her. Now here she was, bedraggled and in a dress Bess didn't recognize, one that didn't fit particularly well.

The nurse burst out laughing. "Well, this is a fine way to great your mam! I'll go find your brother and see if he's got better manners!"

As the nurse left, Bess's mother hugged her again, laughing and crying all at the same time. "No, it isn't my dress," she said. "It's Mrs. Bailey's dress, from across the road."

"Mummy!" Louis came skidding into the room and grabbed his mother around the waist. For a long time, no one said a word. Bess pushed aside the memory of losing Louis at sea. She let the joy and relief of the moment sink in.

Finally, her mother sat back and looked at them both, searchingly. "Bess, Louis. I don't know how to tell you this, after all you've been through." As she paused, Bess's heart constricted with fear. What? What was she afraid to say?

"Our house was hit," her mother continued. "Four days after you left. Everything is gone. Your father and I are fine, but we can't go home."

"What about my old train set?" asked Louis, an odd look on his face.

"It's gone, I'm afraid. I know I promised to look after it, but there was nothing I could do." She sighed. "I'm sorry, Louis."

"That's all right, Mummy," he said brightly. "I've got a new one, see!"

Louis pulled his new train set out from under the bed and started setting it up on the hospital floor.

Bess took a few deep breaths before she trusted herself to speak. She had dreamed of going home, dreamed of the safety of her own bed. All of that time on the overturned lifeboat, she had pictured her mother and father, pictured her house, pictured life before the war. But she realized now there was no way of going back to the time before the war. Life would never be the same.

But they were all alive. That was all that mattered.

"Where will we go?" she finally asked.

"Your father has found us a cottage in a little place called Uley," said her mother gently. "It's inland, in Gloucestershire, and should be safe. We've got a bit saved, and Dad's got hopes of a job as a caretaker at the little local school." Her mother smiled reassuringly, although tears were streaming down her face. "Oh, Bess. We'll be together."

A cottage in the country sounds very peaceful, thought Bess. *Maybe Beth could visit. When the trains are running.* She smiled, weakly.

"Bess. There's another thing," said her mother, drying her eyes. "You've received a lot of letters."

"Letters? What letters?" Bess couldn't imagine who would be writing to her.

"The story that you told the reporter made quite an impact," her mother said. "You've become famous."

"What?"

"You are one of the very few who survived. How you did it is nothing short of a miracle," her mother said. "The story has been in every paper, and they are always talking about you on the radio."

It was a miracle that Bess lived with every day. She didn't understand it at all. She didn't do anything special. All she did was hold on until Albert Gorman came along to rescue her.

"Parents have been writing letters to the newspapers, and they've been forwarded to me," her mother explained.

"Parents?" said Bess.

"Parents of the other children on the boat. They want to know if you can tell them anything about what happened. I think some of them are still hoping that their children might be found." Her mother looked at Louis playing on the floor. "It would be so terrible to lose a child, not to know what happened," she said softly.

Images of the night on the deck flashed into Bess's mind: Children in pajamas, shivering. Abandoned dolls and teddies. Joyce's hand in hers.

"I've been replying to them, explaining that you need time to recover, but I brought you one." Bess looked down at the thin blue envelope in her mother's hand. "It's from a girl who must be about your age. She was a sister of one of the children. I thought it might do you a bit of good to write to her." Her mother's eyes welled up. "They say it sometimes helps to write."

Dear Miss Walder,

I hope you do not mind me writing to you. I read about you in the paper. I was surprised when I read your name, because my sister Gussie mentioned you in her letter to me. She said that you were helping our Lenny to write a letter to our parents.

Gussie had big dreams of a life in Canada and she sounds very happy in her letters. We wouldn't have those letters if it hadn't been for you and your friend helping the little ones to write them.

The letters mean a lot to my parents and me. They're all we've got left of Gussie, Connie, Violet,

Eddie, and Lenny. So I wanted to thank you. For
your kindness.

Sincerely,
Kathleen Grimmond

Beth's hand traced over the fine penmanship of Kathleen's letter. She thought, *you never know how the smallest act might take on huge significance. You never think about how important each day is.*

Dear Kathleen,

I hope you do not mind me calling you Kathleen. I feel I know you already. Gussie spoke of you so fondly. She told me that I would like you because you were smart, and she hoped that we would all meet in Canada one day.

Gussie was a wonderful big sister. Everyone on the boat was impressed by the way that she looked after Connie, Violet, Eddie, and Lenny. She kept them tidy, reminded them of their manners, and stayed with them always. When I last saw her, she had her arms around them all as they waited to get into one of the lifeboats. They were together and she made sure they were not afraid.

I do not know how or why Beth and I survived, when so many others did not. It was very hard, but

I think it is infinitely harder to lose someone you love. When I thought that I had lost my brother, I didn't think I could live with the pain. But I knew that I had to keep going, for my mother and father. I expect you feel the same.

I am grateful to have known Gussie, if only for a short time. I will remember her always.

Your friend, Bess Walder

Chapter Twenty-Five

FRIDAY, SEPTEMBER 20, 1940, 6:32 AM

Friday morning dawned with a warm, sunny wind. As Ken woke up to his third morning in the lifeboat, he heard Officer Cooper and Cadet Critchley synchronizing their watches. "I make it 6:30 AM." said Cooper.

"I have 6:35," said Critchley.

"Let's set it at 6:32," said Cooper.

Six thirty-two. How strange to be caring so much about the time, Ken thought. But he knew that shipboard, even if it was only on a lifeboat, officers kept to routines. Dinner, with its dipper of water, would be at twelve. Supper, with the second dipper of water and tin of milk, would be at six. That was all that mattered, really. That, and storytime.

Gradually, everyone woke up and stretched, to the best of their cramped ability. The lascars scooped small handfuls of seawater into their mouths, swished it around, and spat it out, preparing to say their morning prayers. Ken wondered if they cheated and swallowed. It would feel so good to swallow.

"Our father, who art in heaven."

Father O'Sullivan was still sick with the fever. He lay on the bottom of the boat, leading a morning prayer. Ken watched him fingering his rosary beads constantly. What would happen if he got sicker?

"Give us this day our daily bread."

Ken looked sideways at the priest. He imagined the priest's fever getting worse, imagined him dead, in the bottom of the boat. What would happen then? Would they have to throw him overboard? Would he sink or float?

"And we are grateful for a good wind today," Officer Cooper said, answering the prayer with his own expression of gratitude. He sat in the stern, as he had been doing for three days, holding the tiller. "We could do a hundred miles on a day like this. But we still need to keep a good lookout. Mr. Nagorski, if you would be so good as to take the first rota. Master Sparks, your turn will follow immediately after."

"Look!" Billy was pointing high into the sky. "Sunderland flying ships! Two of them!"

Ken strained his eyes to see two distant figures swoop in the sky.

"Gulls," said Peard, hurling a gob of spit over the side of the boat.

And so the day began. With disappointment.

The sun and wind dried their clothes. Ken's legs ached. His back ached. Everything ached. He tried to enjoy stretching as he manoeuvred over the forward thwart to get to his lookout post in the bow. He felt as though he was wrapped up in a tight sheet, like an Egyptian mummy, unable to move any of his muscles. As he sat in the bow, he tried to will a ship onto the horizon. But there was nothing.

"What shall we sing?" Auntie Mary asked loudly.

"'Run, Rabbit, Run'!" said Fred.

"'Pack up Your Troubles,'" said Derek.

"'There'll Always Be an England,'" said Paul, and he quietly started singing, "There'll always be an England, while there's a country lane."

Auntie Mary joined him. "Wherever there's a cottage small, beside a field of grain."

And then everyone was singing.

There'll always be an England
While there's a busy street,
Wherever there's a turning wheel,
A million marching feet.
Red, white and blue; what does it mean to you?
Surely you're proud, shout it aloud, 'Britons, awake!'
The empire too, we can depend on you. Freedom remains.
These are the chains nothing can break.
There'll always be an England,
And England shall be free

If England means as much to you
As England means to me."

Ken sang loudly, proudly, sending the song out on the waves, out on the wind to the four corners of the world.

Harry the Gunner stood as he sang the last chorus. On the last line he saluted and somersaulted backward into the water, fully dressed, to emerge laughing and spluttering. Everyone—the lascars and even Auntie Mary—applauded.

When dinner was served, Ken was relieved of his lookout post and went back to his perch on the side bench, between the duck hole and the lascars. A biscuit, a half sardine, and a dipper of water.

Billy and Derek gave their biscuits to Auntie Mary. "Can you look after this for me?" said Billy. "I might want it later, but I can't swallow it right now." Ken watched her tuck the biscuits into her pockets. He knew he should eat his, to keep up his strength. But it was like swallowing clay. When no one was looking, he quietly crumbled it and dropped it into the sea.

"Right, who'd like to hear about what's happening to Captain Drummond?" asked Auntie Mary.

"Hurray!" shouted Fred, Howard, Derek, Billy, and Paul. Ken grinned as he moved closer.

"Captain Drummond felt a pistol at his back. 'And so vee meet again, Captain Drummond,' said a strangely familiar voice in a heavy German accent."

Ken felt the sun warming his face. He looked out across the sparkling blue water as Bulldog Drummond battled for his life. It was almost peaceful, sailing along, listening to the adventure.

"Reinholdt turned the key and flung open the heavy steel door.

"'Ah, the room of nails,' exclaimed Drummond.

"'Yes, captain, I've got you now. You'll never escape!' And with an evil laugh, Bulldog Drummond was shoved into the dark room.

"The ropes bit into his wrists. He heard the distant sound of machinery and watched in horror as the wall of nails began to move inexorably toward him. Only seconds stood between him and certain death!"

Silence. "Go on, Auntie Mary," said Billy, nudging her.

"Tomorrow," she said.

"No!"

"The story will continue tomorrow."

Ken looked around. He'd escaped for as long as the story was told. Now he was back in the prison. He wasn't sure which was worse, being cramped or bored. Nothing to do for the rest of the day except look forward to the supper ration. Half a dry biscuit. Half a sardine. A tin of milk. A dipper of water.

Eventually, the sun faded, the stars came twinkling out, and Auntie Mary massaged his legs and feet. She'd started doing that with each of the boys last night, to try and help them get to sleep. Ken could barely feel her working her thumbs down his calf muscles, and onto his puffy, swollen, wet feet. She moved slowly, carefully, but it was as though his feet belonged to someone else's body. Still, it relaxed him.

He lay there looking up at the sky. There was no moon, and the stars covered every part of the sky and were reflected in every part of the water. He was living in a bowl of stars. He felt as though he could reach out and touch them. He connected the dots of the stars, trying to remember what he knew of constellations.

"A shooting star! Make a wish," said Fred.

In the dark of the night, his fourth night on the lifeboat, his wish was pretty obvious.

SATURDAY, SEPTEMBER 21, 1940, 6:30 AM

Another morning. Ken wasn't sure what day it was. It might be Saturday, but he was losing track of time. He lay on his back listening to the morning routines—Officer Cooper and Cadet Critchley synchronizing their watches, the lascars saying their prayers, Paul moaning softly from the duck hole.

Suddenly, Father O'Sullivan shouted, "A whale! Look! A real live whale!"

The priest was standing on the thwart in the middle of the boat. Father O'Sullivan, who had been lying on the bottom of the boat for days, seemingly near death. He was pointing and laughing.

Ken sat up and jerked around to look where he was pointing. Out in the water, about a hundred yards from the right side of the bow, was a sleek black back swimming beside them. It was longer than their entire boat.

"The most magnificent of God's creatures," called out the priest.

"It's huge!" said Derek.

"Look, there's more!" yelled Billy.

Six whales—or was it eight whales?—were swimming beside the boat. The water was churning. The sight filled Ken with awe. It was hard to believe what he was seeing. Spray shot high up in the air from their breathing holes. He wished he could draw them. He longed for his notebook and pencil.

"Man the gears!" Officer Cooper snapped them out of their trance. The shout sent shock waves through the boat. Peard, Critchley, and Purvis all moved to the Fleming gears and started pulling and pushing with all their might.

"We must get away. They could swamp us! Ramjam, get some of your men to work the gears. Tell them the whales will come and scratch their backs on the boat. They could flip us over if we don't move out of here," yelled Cooper.

Everyone responded to the urgency in the officer's voice. Ramjam quickly translated and five lascars grabbed onto the gears. Cooper steered the boat away from the enormous creatures. Ken watched the whales recede into the distance.

When they were out of sight of the whales, a sad calm flooded over the boat. Father O'Sullivan led them in a morning prayer of thanks to God for the wonders of the sea, for the whales. And a thanks for his improved health.

Ken was really sorry to have to leave the whales. They were the first sign of life outside the boat that they had seen in four days.

Dinner was the usual. No one wanted biscuits anymore— they used them as plates for the sardines and then gave them to Auntie Mary for safekeeping. Ken suspected that she was dropping them in the ocean, as he was. He wondered if fish liked hard ship's biscuits. We're feeding the fish, he thought to himself. That's funny. It's as though we are in a large aquarium tank. Maybe that's why the whales came along. Maybe they like hard ship's biscuits.

After dinner, Mr. Nagorski sat on the bottom of the boat pulling soggy pound notes from the pocket of his overcoat. He spread them out meticulously, holding them flat on the wooden footings with spare ship's biscuits.

Ken stared. Such a lot of money.

"What're you doin' that fer?" growled Gunner Peard. "Ain't much use here."

Mr. Nagorski kept at his task. "Not here, no. But I will need it when we are rescued."

Ken suddenly remembered his money. The money that

his stepmother had given him to help him in Canada. What had happened to it? He'd given it to Auntie Mary, as they all had, for safekeeping.

"Auntie Mary ..." he began.

"Auntie Mary, where is *my* money?" interrupted Howard. "I gave it you in the dining room. That first day. I had four and six. I'd been saving it. I'll never have that much again."

"My mum gave me a tanner," said Billy. "She'll be furious if I've lost it. You do have it, don't you, Auntie Mary?"

"What about my good-luck joey?" asked Fred.

"I'm sorry, boys," Auntie Mary held up her hands. "The money was all in a special bag in my cabin in the ship. When the ship was torpedoed, I'm afraid your money went down."

"But I was going to buy my mum a present when I got to Canada," said Derek angrily.

"Will they give it back when we get to Ireland?" asked Howard. "Maybe that Mr. Shakespeare'll give it us back."

"Who?" said Derek.

"Mr. Shakespeare," said Howard. "The one who came on the ship that last day. Before we left Liverpool. 'Member? He checked our life jackets and made sure we knew where our muster station was? He said he was with the government, with CORD."

"You mean CORB," said Ken.

"Yeah, that's it. He sent the letter to my mum and dad saying I could go to Canada. Maybe he'll give us back our money," said Howard.

"My mum's gonna be mad at me ..." sniffed Paul.

Mr. Nagorski stopped putting out his money to dry. He waved his hand for attention.

"Boys, boys. It is very regrettable that Miss Cornish had to leave the moneybag behind on the *Benares*. But of course her attentions were most correctly directed toward her girls and her duties as escort."

Ken felt ashamed that they'd seemed ungrateful to Auntie Mary. Of course she'd been trying to look after her girls. And here she was looking after them, massaging their feet and legs every day, and telling them the Bulldog Drummond stories.

"Do not worry," Mr. Nagorski continued. "When we get back, I will make up to each of you the money you have lost."

Ken's jaw dropped. He and the rest of the boys looked at Mr. Nagorski in stunned silence. He'd known that Mr. Nagorski was different. He sat so straight every day in his homburg hat, overcoat, and gloves. He shined his shoes every morning, using a bit of a handkerchief that he kept in his pocket. And he spoke with an accent. But Ken hadn't known that he was rich. He must be really rich, thought Ken. He's probably a millionaire.

"Thank you very much, sir," said Howard, speaking for them all. "Thank you very much, indeed." Howard paused. "Do you think we'll be taken to Canada or be in Ireland when we are rescued?"

Chapter Twenty-Six

The dark of the night lifted, but cold and rain settled in. Critchley and Cooper synchronized their watches. The lascars muttered their morning prayers. Father O'Sullivan said grace. The morning water and meal were passed around.

Ken wasn't sure he could swallow any of the sardine. He held the water in his mouth as long as he could before swallowing it. He held the sardine in his hand and lay back down in the boat.

He was vaguely aware of Harry the Gunner going for his morning swim in the icy water. How could anyone swim on a day like today? He thought he heard him whistling "Run, Rabbit, Run." How could anyone whistle while they were swimming?

The rain began to pelt down. He opened his mouth

where he lay, hoping to catch some.

"Let's try to collect up some of this," said Officer Cooper. "Critchley, Purvis, loosen those ropes on the tarp. Make a hollow in it to collect water."

Cadet Critchley and Steward Purvis picked their way through the tangled bodies of the lascars and worked their way to the bow. Ken scrunched up on the side bench so they could set up the tarp to catch rainwater. A small pool of water grew in the centre of the plastic covering. Everyone watched eagerly.

Purvis scooped some into the water dipper and tasted it.

"Phew," he spat it out. "Salt. Solid salt." He looked around at the disappointed faces. "The tarp is covered in sea spray. We can't drink this. Sorry," he muttered as he dumped the water into the sea.

Ken felt ice hitting his head. The rain was turning to hail. He moved off the bench and crouched under the tarp with the others, trying not to get hit. As he watched, icicles formed on the gunwales. He reached out and broke one off. He turned to Howard, who did the same. They looked at each other as they tucked the icy sticks in their mouths. It tasted a bit salty, but then everything did. It felt wonderful to hold the cold ice in his mouth. It made the hailstorm worthwhile.

He looked out over the frozen water. Small icebergs dotting the horizon. Growlings, Father O'Sullivan had called them. He remembered the story of the *Titanic*. Were those icebergs big enough to sink a lifeboat?

"I've got a treat for all of you today," announced Purvis from the stern. "Cadet Critchley and I are going to hand out something very special with your noon meal."

This got everyone's attention.

"What is it? What have you got?" Ken couldn't imagine what he could possibly have for them. He wished it was ice cream. But he knew that was impossible. What could it be?

"You'll just have to wait and see. When it's noon," said Purvis, grinning through his rough beard.

"While we wait for our treat," said Auntie Mary to all of the boys, "I want you to tell me what is the first thing you are going to eat when you get home? What's your favourite food?"

"Bangers an' mash," said Ken, without a moment's hesitation. "With a bit of fried onion on the side. Lovely fat bangers."

"I'm gonna have fish 'n' chips!" said Billy.

"Yeah," said Derek, "Fish 'n' chips is my favourite."

"Roast beef!" said Howard.

"With Yorkshire pudding," said Fred.

"A chocolate Swiss roll for tea," said Paul weakly.

"If we land in Ireland, maybe they'll give us Irish stew!" said Derek.

"Or if it's Scotland, it'll be Scotch broth," said Fred.

"Or if it's Iceland, they'll give us ice cream!" laughed Howard.

"What about you, Auntie Mary? What will you have?" asked Ken.

"Oh, I think I'll have a lovely bit of roast chicken with bread sauce," said Auntie Mary. "And a nice cold sarsaparilla."

"Sarsaparilla!" All of the boys pounced on the idea.

"Sarsaparilla is my absolute favourite," said Derek. "Ice-cold sarsaparilla. Father O'Sullivan," he called out, "if I pray hard enough, will God give me a sarsaparilla when I get home?"

The ice storm passed. The day settled into being grey, cold, and rainy. When dinner came, the surprise was worth the waiting. Ken couldn't believe his eyes when Cadet Critchley handed him a sliver of canned peach. Probably not more than an eighth of a whole peach, but it was a sliver that slid down his parched throat. A sliver that tasted like the best candy in the world. A sliver that made a fat tear roll down his face. It tasted that good. After the peach slice, Critchley poured a spoonful of peach juice into their empty milk tins. Ken took tiny sips, making it last as long as possible. This *was* a special day.

After dinner, Ken lay in the duck hole, napping. He wasn't sleeping exactly, but he wasn't really awake either. He was trying to hold the memory of the sticky sweetness of the peach in his mouth. In his dreaming state, he thought he heard Mr. Nagorski say "Ship ahoy."

"Ship!" shouted Signalman Mayhew, with increased excitement. "It's a ship."

Ken jerked his head out of the duck hole. Sure enough, away in the distance, off to the left, through the rain, it looked like—could it really be?—a small cargo vessel.

"Man the Fleming gears," said Officer Cooper and Mr. Nagorski, Peard, Purvis, and Critchley all started to work the handles.

Everyone was awake and moving now. Rescue! Finally, they were going to go home. Home to bangers and mash. Home to fish and chips. Home to roast beef and Yorkshire pudding. Home to sarsaparilla.

"They can't see us this far out," shouted Officer Cooper above the sound of the rain. "Mayhew, set off our flares. We've got to move faster. Throw that covering away—it's just slowing us down."

Ken leapt up and helped Ramjam throw the cover for the duck hole into the sea. They certainly wouldn't need it any more. Mayhew set off one flare. Up it went with a zing, high into the air, leaving a trail of coloured smoke.

They were closing in. It was a steamer. It looked like it might have been a liner once. A couple of the lascars took off their turbans, which they never did, and waved them in the air. Everyone was calling out, hoping to be heard above the rain, above the waves.

Mayhew set off their last flare. "Pull harder," shouted

Officer Cooper. Ken could just make out men walking on the deck of the ship. He took off his pyjama top and waved it with all his might.

But suddenly, horrifyingly, the ship turned sideways. Her propellers started. She began to move away from them.

"No! Wait! Stop!! Help!" Everyone was screaming now. Everyone waving.

But it was no use. The ship was moving quickly.

And then it was gone. Just as quickly as it had appeared, it disappeared over the horizon.

Ken felt the sorrow of forty-six people. Forty-six pairs of arms hanging uselessly by the sides of forty-six bodies. Forty-six pairs of eyes staring in disbelief.

Slowly, forty-six people sat down into their well-worn places on the boat. The sound of the wind and rain was all around them, but there was utter silence inside each of them.

Harry the Gunner was the first to speak. "Well, what're ye looking so black about? Don'cha see? This means we're in the shippin' lanes. Where there's one ship, there'll be another along soon enough. Just you wait 'n' see."

Ken watched Mr. Nagorski work his way to the stern, gracefully moving through the lascars and over the thwarts, to talk to Officer Cooper. He had learned that the adults on the boat sometimes had things to say to each other that they didn't say to the rest of them. He moved as close as he could get to the stern by crawling under the side benches. He strained his ears to listen.

"Not sure," Officer Cooper was saying quietly. "I could have sworn they saw us."

"But surely," said Mr. Nagorski, "surely if they saw us they would have known that we were from the *Benares*."

"All I can think is they thought we were a decoy. There's a rumour going around that U-boats are using lifeboats as decoys. They lure unsuspecting ships to rescue them, and then fire torpedoes. They might have thought we were a trap."

"But anyone in these waters would be on the lookout for us. They would have been told to find us," Mr. Nagorski's voice rose.

"I'm afraid no one is looking for us, Mr. Nagorski. Our only hope is to reach Ireland."

Mr. Nagorski narrowed his eyes as he stared hard at Officer Cooper. "And how close are we?"

"I don't know," said Cooper, quietly. "Still a few days, I think."

As night came on, the winds picked up.

"Looks like we're heading into a storm," said Cooper. "Critchley, let's get this sail down so we can ride it out."

No sooner had he said this than the boat started to pitch

and roll in the waves. Peard cast out the sea anchor.

"Lie low! Out of the storm!" shouted Cooper. "Hang on tightly to whatever you can!"

The rain burst on them like an angry beast. The wind whipped the waves into foaming towers. The storm picked up energy. Ken remembered the very first night, when the *Benares* had gone down. He wasn't sure he could face that again.

His overcoat was sodden and he was quickly drenched to the skin. They'd thrown away the duck-hole cover, so there was nothing to protect them. Ken saw Purvis bailing furiously with their one bucket. Mr. Nagorski was using his hat to bail. The lascars were trying to use their hands.

Ken jammed himself under the side bench. Auntie Mary moved with Paul to the centre of the boat and wrapped him around one of the Fleming handles. She lay down behind him, twisting to hold him secure. The boat rose high in the air and came crashing down. Ken felt the waves twist and shake the thin planks. Surely the boat couldn't take all of this.

Had they come all of this way to be capsized now?

He was scared. The fear started to take over his whole body and he began to shake. He was tired of this adventure and wanted to be home. He could hear Billy and Derek crying weakly. It was like the first night in the boat, so long ago. A whole other lifetime. How long had they been at sea?

He thought about how good the sliver of peach had tasted at dinner.

Ken cried. For the first time he realized they weren't going to make it home.

Chapter Twenty-Seven

MONDAY, SEPTEMBER 23, 1940, 5:30 AM

A faint roll of thunder sounded in the distance. Ken slowly opened his eyes. It was grey and the rain fell lightly, but it was morning, and the storm had passed. He watched Auntie Mary uncurl herself from around the Fleming handles. He watched her gently shake Paul, and then smile in his face. He watched Ramjam walk among the lascars, shaking them, speaking to them quietly. They seemed a solid mass in the bottom of the boat. A mass of brown men in ragged clothing with no muscle or movement. He watched Officer Cooper at the far end of the boat, steering quietly.

Auntie Mary crawled over the lascars to the bow. "You all right, Ken?" she whispered. He nodded slowly. She moved along to Billy. "Billy?" Ken watched him nod. He watched Auntie Mary make her way to each of the boys.

Everyone answered her in a quiet voice. Ken saw her look back at Officer Cooper and give him a small wave.

She was checking to make sure we're all still alive, he thought with a shock.

Mr. Nagorski dipped his handkerchief in the sea and washed his face. He dipped it again, and wiped off his shoes. Then he made his way to the bow and together he and Auntie Mary started the new morning ritual— massaging feet. Ken liked it when Mr. Nagorski massaged him. His hands were soft, but sure. Ken felt a calmness pass into his body.

When the morning meal came around, no one felt like eating. No one even wanted the tinned milk. *I'd trade all of the food on this boat for another dipper of water*, Ken thought. He watched the lascars' round eyes follow the dipper as it went around the boat. *They're thinking the same thing as I am. They want more. They want my water.*

The day was long, quiet, and still. No one seemed to have the energy to talk. The routines continued. In Auntie Mary's Bulldog story, Drummond walked in lush gardens in Devon, where there were flowers that Ken had never heard of and couldn't picture.

As dusk fell, someone said, "Land," but no one really believed it.

"Really, I think it is," said Mr. Nagorski. "There. That big lump." Ken sat up and strained his eyes in the direction he was pointing. It certainly looked like a crest of land off in the distance—a smudge on the horizon. But they had seen so many odd things. Billy was always seeing ships in the clouds on the horizon.

As darkness fell, Signal Mayhew thought he saw lights.

"It looks like anti-aircraft fire," he offered.

"It could be," said Officer Cooper, but he sounded doubtful. "We'll try to hold our course and see if we can see it any better in the daylight." All they could do was wait out the night huddled under the two sodden blankets.

All they could do was wait.

TUESDAY, SEPTEMBER 24, 1940, 5:30 AM

There was no island, no land, no faint smudge on the horizon. Nothing but bright sun and sparkling water as far as the eye could see.

Ken's tongue was sticking to the roof of his mouth. He wasn't sure that even if he had some water he'd be able to swallow it. His eyes burned. It hurt less if he kept them closed. His lips were split and caked with salt.

It was very still in the boat. Ken could hear Cooper and Critchley synchronizing watches, but no one else was moving. The boat was just drifting. No one put the sail up. No one was bothering with the Fleming gears. As the sun rose, it began to burn Ken's skin.

Out of the corner of his eye, he saw movement. One of

the lascars began to peel himself away from the group, disturbing everyone as he started to get up. He seemed very awake all of the sudden.

Suddenly, he was screaming. Ken couldn't understand any of the words, couldn't make sense of the sounds. The man stood up and pulled off his long cotton shirt. He kept screaming as he stood on the gunwales of the boat and threw himself into the water.

Everyone sat stunned. Was he pretending to be Harry the Gunner? Was he making some kind of joke? Ken stared as the waves pushed the man up and down in the water, his arms flailing as he yelled incoherently.

And then he was gone.

It felt as though everyone in the boat was holding their breath as they waited for him to reappear.

But he didn't. He was gone. As though he had never been there.

Suddenly, the other lascars all started screaming at once. They yelled in a mix of sounds, pointing at the ocean. Ramjam stood among them, speaking calmly, trying to sooth them. Their voices rose to a fevered pitch that sent currents of fear through Ken.

Officer Cooper stood up in the stern of the boat and all eyes turned to him. He spoke to everyone in a loud clear voice.

"The lascar lost his mind. Probably from drinking saltwater. There is nothing any of us could have done."

Nothing they could have done. The man was alive, he lost his mind, now he was dead and gone. Vanished. As though he had never been there.

Would the salty ice that he'd sucked on the other day make him lose his mind too, Ken wondered? Would he jump into the water and disappear like the lascar?

The lascars chattered, clearly disturbed, as Ramjam translated Officer Cooper's message. Ken realized that he hadn't really thought much about the lascars in the last few days. He'd been more worried about himself. Now he looked at them and saw how thin they were. Their cotton uniforms were no protection again the cold. They must have been freezing during the hailstorm. Their bare feet were swollen and covered in sores.

Mr. Nagorski worked his way to the stern to talk with Purvis and Ramjam. Then the three of them negotiated their way to the bow, to the supply cupboard in the hold. Purvis pulled out a first-aid kit and a bottle of dark brown liquid. "Iodine," said Purvis, handing the bottle to Mr. Nagorski.

"Tell them I am going to paint their feet," Ken heard Mr. Nagorski say to Ramjam. "Tell them that this bottle of medicine will make them better. It will sting a little bit, but it will make them better. Tell them it will make them all better."

Ramjam spoke calmly to the lascars. Their eyes were encrusted with salt, the same as Ken's. Maybe worse. He saw them give small nods to Mr. Nagorski.

Mr. Nagorski sat down in the middle of the boat among the lascars. He uncorked the bottle and pulled out a wire handle with a bit of cotton at the end. He began to carefully paint one of the lascars' feet with the brown liquid. The lascar winced, but held his foot steady. Everyone in the boat watched.

Slowly, a feeling of calm came over the boat as Mr. Nagorski painted thirty-three pairs of swollen and peeling feet. Ken knew how much he liked Mr. Nagorski massaging his feet. He hoped that the lascars felt the same way about getting their feet painted with medicine.

After the noon dipper of water, Billy leaned over to Auntie Mary. She was lying on the bottom of the boat.

"Auntie Mary. It's time for another Bulldog Drummond story."

"I'm not sure I can," she said quietly.

"Please, Auntie Mary. We have to know where Bulldog is. We have to know what he is doing," Billy pleaded.

Her voice was barely above a whisper, so all of the boys lay down close beside her. There were Nazi soldiers and spies. Bulldog Drummond faced certain death in a foreign prison. But sometimes Auntie Mary said things that didn't make sense. There were whales and little girls who played the piano. One minute Bulldog Drummond was fighting a duel with an evil duke. The next he was conducting a symphony in Vienna. Ken just listened and followed along as best he could.

When she finished Billy asked quietly, "Auntie Mary, when is that other ship coming back to get us?"

The day was still. There was a soft breeze, but nothing to fill out the sail. The sound of water lapped gently again the boat. There was deep silence at the evening meal that night.

"Tomorrow," began Steward Purvis. He cleared his throat. "Tomorrow I am going to have to halve your water ration. We want to make sure that we have enough to get to Ireland. So you'll only have water with the evening meal tomorrow."

Ken heard the words, but only barely understood them. There was no point in getting upset. There was nothing to be done.

The dark came on. A clear night, filled with stars. Just as he was drifting off to sleep, Ken heard a funny sound beside him. It started as a low rumbling, muttering sort of sound. He realized that it was Paul talking to himself. But suddenly Paul started screaming with a force that seemed beyond anything Ken could imagine.

"I'm dying! Get me out! Stop! Stop! NO, I CAN'T! PLEASE!"

Father O'Sullivan crawled over Ken to get to Paul. He squeezed between them and tried to lie next to him on the floor of the boat.

"HELP! STOP! DON'T MAKE ME! I DON'T WANT TO DIE!"

The priest put his arms around Paul, trying to hold him,

to speak gently in his ear. But Paul was thrashing, trying to get his pyjamas off. Auntie Mary lay down on the other side of Paul and together they tried to hold Paul down.

"Our Father, who art in Heaven," the priest began.

"Lullabye, and goodnight," Auntie Mary began to sing in a strained and wild voice.

"I DON'T WANT TO DIE!" Ken watched in horror as Paul lay screaming, kicking, and smashing at the priest and Auntie Mary. Had Paul lost his mind, like the lascar? Was he going to jump overboard, too?

Everyone in the boat was wide awake now. Mr. Nagorski made his way over, grabbed the blanket off Ken, and pushed it down over Paul, practically sitting on him. Auntie Mary began to massage his legs. "Soft and warm is your bed, Close your eyes and rest your head," she sang. Paul screamed louder.

"I AM DYING! I NEED WATER!" Paul yelled. Ken felt a wave of fear and anger roll into the boat. He felt like he could taste it. His heart started to pound.

The lascars started talking. There was anger in their voices. "You must quiet the boy," said Officer Cooper from the stern. "You must make him stop."

"I DON'T WANT TO DIE!" screamed Paul.

"What's this? What's this?" Harry the Gunner stepped over the lascars and made his way from the stern to the bow. He stood over Paul. "What's all this noise?"

"WATER! I NEED WATER! I'M THIRSTY!" screamed Paul.

"We're all thirsty," said Gunner Peard steadily. "We all want water. You'll get your share tomorrow, same as everyone else," he said loudly.

"MY FEET ARE COLD!!" screamed Paul.

Peard looked at Paul's bare feet. "Nice way to treat a kid," he said to Auntie Mary. "Give me your jacket," he said to her.

Auntie Mary slowly took off her jacket and handed it to Peard. She sat there shivering in a thin, torn camisole. Peard wrapped her jacket around Paul's feet. He took a piece of rope out of his pocket and looped it around Paul's ankles, holding the jacket in place. "There," he said, "you warm now?"

"MY FEET ARE COLD!!" Paul screamed.

"Critchley, toss me your coat," Gunner Peard called back to the cadet in the stern.

"MY FEET ARE COLD!!" Paul screamed again.

Everyone watched as Cadet Critchley took off his coat and passed it up through the boat to Gunner Peard, who wrapped the coat around Paul's feet and tied it on over Auntie Mary's jacket.

"There. Any better?"

"MY FEET ARE COLD!!" said Paul.

"NO, THEY'RE NOT!" Peard sounded so angry that Ken thought he might hit Paul. Ken was terrified that Peard might suddenly start hitting all of them. He lay stiff as a board beside Paul, not daring to move a muscle.

"Your feet're wrapped up properly now and they're warm as toast." Peard glared down into Paul's face. "Now—are your feet warm?"

"MY FEET—!"

"BE QUIET!" Peard's voice boomed out over the empty ocean. "Don't let me hear another sound out of you till morning. No more of this yelling out." Peard barked at Paul. "Now—are your feet warm?"

"… Yes …" said Paul.

"Then you'll be all right till the morning."

Peard grumbled as he made his way back to his spot in the stern. Ken felt Paul's body begin to relax beside him. He felt his own breath rise and fall. He listened to the sound of the water smacking the side of the boat.

WEDNESDAY, SEPTEMBER 25, 1940

He was finding it difficult to tell the difference between being awake and being asleep. He knew if there were stars blinking, it must be night. And if the sun was blazing overhead, it must be day.

So it must be day. Morning, he judged. The boat rocked a bit and he heard a splash. Harry the Gunner, doing his regular morning swim around the boat. He heard him go around the boat twice. He felt him haul himself back into the boat. A mist of water sprayed him as the gunner shook the water off of himself, as he did every morning.

The boat bobbed along in the water, carried slowly by whatever current caught it. No one had worked the Fleming gears in two days. There was no wind for the sail.

"I've got a special treat for you today." Ken was lying in the bottom of the boat. He heard Purvis speaking hoarsely from the stern. "A slice of canned pear."

Ken sat up. Pieces of pear were handed around. Ken took his and put it in his mouth. He tried to chew. He watched Paul lying beside him spit his out. He made himself swallow.

The boat was very still. Ken was afraid that if he lay down again he might not get back up. He looked at Paul, his feet still wrapped from the night before. He'd heard Auntie Mary say he had trench foot. Ken didn't know exactly what that was, but he gathered it was serious. His own feet were a soft, swollen, peeling mass. He wasn't sure he could walk on them. Not that he had anywhere to walk.

He gazed dully out over the empty ocean. He looked up into the clear sky. He saw ...

"A plane," he croaked.

His breath came in short gasps. He tried to make himself heard.

"Plane."

No one moved. Ken gathered every ounce of energy he had in his body. He stood up. The boat rocked gently. He felt as though everything was happening in slow motion. He spoke, in a loud, clear voice.

"Look. There. Is. A. Plane. LOOK!"

He pointed. Mr. Nagorski was beside him.

Ken's breathing quickened. Time sped up, but still everyone moved in slow motion. He ripped off his shirt and started to wave it madly.

"It's a Sunderland! A Sunderland Flying Ship! OVER HERE! OVER HERE!" Ken screamed.

He felt movement in the boat. The lascars turned their heads. They looked up. Officer Cooper stood up in the stern. Cadet Critchley and Signalman Mayhew stood up beside him. Everyone raised their heads. The boat seemed to hold its breath.

Suddenly, Ken could hear the buzz he'd been waiting for, the drone of an engine. Now all eyes were fixed on the sky. And the boat exploded in the noise as everyone started waving and screaming.

"STOP!" shouted Officer Cooper. "It might be a German plane. Everyone lie down! Lie low!"

It was a direct order from their captain. No one obeyed him. "Over here! Over here!" they shouted.

Ken waved his shirt and yelled, "It's not German! It's a Sunderland!" Ken knew that plane as well as he knew his own house.

The lascars ripped off their turbans and waved them in the air. The plane was definitely coming toward them. It had seen them.

Suddenly Signalman Mayhew yelled, "They signalled!

They just signalled with their Aldis lamp. They are on our side!"

Mayhew grabbed two brightly coloured turbans from the lascars and began to respond to the plane with semaphore signals.

"C-I-T-Y-O-F-B-E-N-A-R-E-S," said Mayhew as he signalled.

The plane was close enough that they could see the pilot in his helmet.

Billy and Derek began flashing a signal using the sun's reflection off their empty milk tins. Three short, three long, three short. The only code they knew: s.o.s.

"We're gonna to fly home!" laughed Howard.

Another series of flashes from the Aldis lamp. Suddenly the plane was turning.

"NO!" Everyone in the boat screamed.

"SILENCE!" shouted Officer Cooper. He turned to Mayhew. "What did they say?"

"They can't land, sir. The waves are too rough. But they've signalled ahead." Mayhew's voice shook as he turned to speak to everyone in the boat. "They're sending another plane. It will be here soon."

The silence was deep and tense.

I don't think I can stand it if the other plane doesn't come, thought Ken. *I think I will have to jump into the sea, just like that lascar.*

They waited.

And waited.

Barely breathing. Watching the sky with anticipation.

"There! There it is!" Ken shouted. Far in the distance he could see a spot getting larger, coming straight at them.

The plane circled around them. Ken waved to the co-pilot, who was leaning out of the window taking a photograph. Flashes of light sent messages. Mayhew translated.

"They're saying that there are too many of us to take in the plane," said Mayhew. "They're sending a ship. A destroyer. It is two hours away. They'll guide it to us."

Suddenly, a huge parcel dropped from the plane. It was attached to a life jacket and it dropped right beside the lifeboat. Harry the Gunner dove into the water to bring it over to the side, as the plane flew off.

Purvis and Mayhew lifted the package into the boat and opened it. Canned peaches and pears, soups, fish, beans in tomato sauce—hot in a thermos!

"It's a feast!" cried Fred. Billy, Derek, and Howard were laughing hysterically. The boat felt electrified.

"But there's no extra water. So you will only get the usual dipperful," said Purvis. "There will be lots of water once we are rescued. But we have no guarantee of how long that will be."

Ken didn't care. He greedily drank all of the juice from a can of pears. As far as he was concerned someone else could have the pears. All he wanted was the juice.

Mayhew pulled out a mouth organ and started to play "Pack up your troubles in your old kit bag." Everyone, even the lascars, joined in on "Smile, smile, smile." Ken felt giddy. A small part of him wondered if this was real. But he smiled and sang and pushed away his fear.

What's the use of worrying?
It never was worthwhile.
So, pack up your troubles in your old kit bag,
And smile, smile, smile.

When they finally saw the ship in the distance, Purvis gave everyone a last dipper of water. Before they knew it, the ship was upon them. It was barrelling toward them and waves began to rock the lifeboat wildly from side to side.

Mayhew quickly signalled. "I am asking them to slow down and make the water quiet. To let us come to them, rather than them trying to come to us," he said to Officer Cooper. "We don't want to get swamped and drown now!" he said.

Ken watched the destroyer slow and move in a circular path, well away from the lifeboat. Cadet Critchley, Harry the Gunner, Mr. Nagorski, and Ramjam worked the Fleming gears while Officer Cooper steered the lifeboat to the side of the ship. Ken looked up at the deck of the destroyer. It was filled with crewmen all waving and laughing and cheering.

Ken felt a moment of panic. The ship was enormous. After being alone on the ocean for so long, his perspective had changed entirely. It was as though a whole city had suddenly materialized out of thin air. The *Benares* was this big, he thought. On the side of the ship was painted the name HMS *Anthony*.

"Say a prayer of thanks to St. Anthony," said Father O'Sullivan, "The patron saint of lost things."

The crew of the *Anthony* dropped rope ladders over the side, down to the lifeboat. Ken was completely overwhelmed. All of this sound, all of this activity. He had no idea what he was supposed to do. He sat inert, watching four sailors climb from the deck down the ladders to the lifeboat. They, too, seemed suddenly unsure. They couldn't fit in the lifeboat. There was no place for them to stand, other than on the gunwales. "You've been in this boat for eight days?" They stared.

"Seven days, nineteen hours." said Officer Cooper. "Thank you for rescuing us."

WEDNESDAY, SEPTEMBER 25, 1940, 4:30 PM

Strong arms lifted Ken into a large, heavy net. The net was hoisted up and onto the deck of the ship. *I'm just like a large fish*, thought Ken. Behind him he could hear Paul screaming, "Don't leave me! Don't leave me out here!"

When Ken arrived on deck, he tried to walk, but he felt searing pain shoot through his body and he screamed as he collapsed. A sailor lifted him over his shoulder. Out of the corner of his eye he saw Harry the Gunner climb up the rope ladder and leap onto the deck.

Ken was taken into a cabin. The sailor gently took off his salt-encrusted clothes, and put him into a clean sailor's uniform. It was miles too big, but it felt wonderful. Then he was carried into the officer's mess and given a steaming mug of tea, warm milk, and thin porridge. All of the boys were there, except Paul. He'd been taken straight to the infirmary.

A group of sailors sat around the boys, smiling from ear to ear.

"Sir," Ken said to the closest, as he sipped his delicious sweet tea. "Sir, are you taking us to Canada now?"

"No, son," said the sailor, looking at Ken very seriously, "we are taking you home. You are going home."

Chapter Twenty-Eight

FRIDAY, SEPTEMBER 27, 1940

Torpedoed Evacuees Back from the Dead—
Thousand to One Chance Comes Off in Mid-
Atlantic.
　　—*News of the World*

The news of the rescue was wired ahead and all of England
cheered. It was a miracle. Forty-five people, among them
six children, were "back from the dead."

It took two days for the HMS *Anthony* to reach Gourock
in Scotland. Ken stood on the deck with the others, grinning
from ear to ear in his overcoat, and proudly wearing an
HMS *Anthony* sailor's cap. There was a huge crowd of
people at the dock.

"Why're they there?" Ken asked Mr. Nagorski.

"Because of you, Ken. You, Howard, Fred, Derek, Billy,
and Paul. The whole country is cheering," he said with a
soft smile.

Ken saw people laughing, crying, and waving flags. It was such a confusion of noise and activity. Suddenly, he was hoisted in the air and plunked on the shoulders of one of the sailors.

"I know you're still havin' a bit a trouble with yer feet," said the sailor. "Best I carry you down."

He looked around and saw Howard, Fred, Derek, and Billy in the air as well. Paul was still in the infirmary. His feet were in pretty bad shape. Auntie Mary had said that Paul and Father O'Sullivan would be carried out on stretchers.

Ken was home. Seeing land, real, solid land, was unbelievable. He laughed and waved.

Photographers' lightbulbs were flashing all around them as they made their way down the gangplank. Reporters starting shouting up to Ken.

"How does it feel to be back in Britain?"

"What was the hardest thing about being in the lifeboat?"

"Did you ever give up hope?"

On and on the questions came, fast and furious. *All I ever did was survive*, thought Ken. *I couldn't have done that without Auntie Mary, Steward Purvis, or Harry the Gunner.*

Mr. Shakespeare, the man from the government, was there at the bottom of the gangplank.

"Welcome home, boys! We didn't think we'd ever see you again," he said.

"We were right where we were supposed to be!" said Howard. "Where are the others?"

Mr. Shakespeare looked nervous.

Why, thought Ken. *What is he hiding?*

"The HMS *Hurricane* rescued the survivors from the *Benares*. Apparently, it just missed you lot. The ship arrived here last week."

"Last week!" said Fred. "What must my mum have thought?"

"Well," said Mr. Shakespeare, "I had to send your mummies and daddies telegrams last week. To tell them you'd died at sea. They've already had a big memorial for you all," he said with a small chuckle.

Fred roared with laughter. "Won't they be surprised now!"

"Surprised and very, very happy," said Mr. Shakespeare. "I'm looking forward to writing new telegrams with this good news!"

Ken wondered how it would feel to go home. He was looking forward to seeing Mollie. He hoped his stepmother wouldn't mind him coming back. He hoped she wouldn't be mad at him for ruining his father's overcoat. He was still wearing it, but it was ripped and salt-stained.

"A week ago the whole country was angry about the *Benares* being torpedoed. But today everyone is celebrating you boys making it back! We're going to take you over to the very best hotel in Gourock. You *Anthony* boys are a miracle!"

Anthony boys. Lost boys. Found, thought Ken.

The next few days were filled with celebrations. The Lord Provost of Glasgow gave them kilts, sporrans, and gold badges with a crest of arms on them that entitled them to a free meal, any time they were in Glasgow, for the rest of their lives.

But Ken and the others could only just barely walk. Their stomachs couldn't handle more than a few bites of food at a time. They were exhausted. The Lord Provost took them to his hunting lodge, so they could get away from the reporters and get a bit of rest. It was there that Ken asked the question they'd all been avoiding.

"Sir, why *is* everyone making such a fuss of us?"

"Because we're all so glad to see you home, and alive. Because we lost so many others," said the Lord Provost.

"What do you mean?" said Howard. "Didn't they all come home on the *Hurricane*?"

The Lord Provost looked at them. "Do you mean no one's told you?"

"Told us what?" asked Fred.

"About the *Hurricane*? About the survivors?"

They all stared at him dumbly.

"There were only fourteen children on the *Hurricane*, only seven of them from the CORB program."

Ken was dumbfounded. Only seven seavacuees? Out of ninety?

"Alan?" asked Derek.

"Peter?" asked Billy quietly.

"I'm afraid your brothers didn't make it, boys," said the Lord Provost.

"Terry?" asked Ken. The Lord Provost shook his head slowly.

For a long time, no one said anything. Tears bounced down Derek's nose. The Lord Provost put his arm around Billy as he cried softly.

"We thought everyone else had been saved ... that it was just that our boat had been missed," said Fred eventually.

Howard turned to Ken. "I'd always assumed that we were the unlucky ones."

Images of their time on the *Benares* flooded Ken's mind. Children playing tag in the playroom. The football games. The tea party. The laughter.

"Looks like we were the lucky ones," said Ken, quietly.

A week later, the boys were well enough to go home. Ken knew his father couldn't make the journey all the way to Scotland, so he asked Fred's parents if he could travel back to London with them. He could work his way back to Wembley from Euston station on his own. He stood in the hotel lobby with the others, trying to figure out how to say goodbye.

Auntie Mary held him, wordlessly.

Officer Cooper was in the lobby. So were Signalman Mayhew, Cadet Critchley, Steward Purvis, and Harry the Gunner.

Suddenly a familiar, formal voice cut through the emotion.

"I have not forgotten my promise."

The boys all turned to look as Mr. Nagorski strode up to them. He had on a new overcoat and homburg hat and fresh shining shoes. He was carrying a soft leather wallet.

"It is time to reimburse you for your lost funds." Ken looked at Howard and Fred. They were grinning ear to ear. "I would like to honour each of you for your bravery and valour," continued Mr. Nagorski, "so I am going to give you double the amount, plus a little to round it to the nearest pound. So much easier than carrying coins."

The boys all shrieked. Twice as much?!

"That means I'll be going home richer than when I left!" laughed Ken.

When Ken finally got home, Wembley was decorated with flags. All of the neighbours were out on the streets cheering as he walked up from the tube station to his flat. His stepmother hugged him. Hard.

"It broke our hearts to get that telegram. To read that you'd died," she said with feeling. "Your old room's all ready for you."

"Mollie'll stay in the box room. Give you a bit of space. Growin' lad needs a bit a space," his father added.

Of course, the war wasn't over. There were still nightly

bombing raids. There was still fear. The horror of war would continue for another five long years. There would be many, many deaths.

But the children who survived from the *City of Benares* disaster recovered from their injuries and lived through the war.

When he was old enough, Ken joined the navy.

Bess visited Beth, where she met Beth's brother Geoff. And when she was old enough, she married him.

Sonia grew up to become a schoolteacher. After the war, when she was old enough, she sailed across the ocean to Canada to teach in British Columbia.

And for over seventy years, on every September 17, they remembered the children who did not come home.

Afterword

This book is based on true events. The children and adults are based on real people.

However, this is a work of fiction. While I have included survivors' memories and some of their remembered dialogue, I have created imaginary scenes and personalities. I have conflated incidents, and had to leave many people out of the story.

The facts remain the same. There were ninety seavacuees travelling on the *City of Benares*, accompanied by ten volunteer escorts. There were ninety-one fee-paying passengers at the other end of the ship, among them ten children. On September 17, 1940, at 10:03 PM, when the ship was 650 nautical miles west of Ireland, torpedoes were fired from a German U-boat, *U-48*. The first missed. The second hit the SS *City of Benares* during a force 10 storm. A third hit the SS *Marina*.

Commander Bleichrodt of *U-48* later stated that he had

no idea that children were aboard the ship. He assumed that given the large escort, the ship was of great military importance. The SS *City of Benares* took thirty-one minutes to sink after being struck by the torpedo.

Almost all of the *Benares'* lifeboats flipped over on launch, due either to faulty mechanisms or because of the violence of the storm. Most of the 406 passengers and crew were thrown into the ocean. Captain Nicoll went down with the ship.

The HMS *Winchelsea*, the lead escort, had left the *Benares* convoy twenty-four hours before the attack. It was assumed that the *Benares* was in safe water, so the *Winchelsea* left to escort an inbound ship carrying much-needed supplies from Halifax to England. The *Winchelsea* was more than two hundred miles away when the *Benares* was hit.

HMS *Hurricane H06*, was three hundred miles away. At approximately 11:00 PM on Tuesday, September 17, the *Hurricane* received a message to proceed with "utmost dispatch to position 56.43N 21.15 W, where survivors are reported in boats." It took eighteen hours for the destroyer to get to the disaster site, travelling through the storm, pushing the ship's engines to their limits to get there as soon as possible. They arrived at the site of the disaster at 1:00 PM on Wednesday, September 18.

Fifty-one of the original group of ninety-one fee-paying passengers died, including three children. Of the forty-nine British crewmen and convoy staff who set sail on September

13, twenty-three died. One hundred and one of the original one hundred and sixty-six lascars died.

The greatest percentage of the death toll was paid by the seavacuee children: seventy-seven of the ninety CORB children died. Six of their ten volunteer escorts died.

The lifeboat from the *SS Marina* that set sail to Ireland after leaving lifeboat 12 reached an island off the coast on Wednesday September 25. The sailors were weak, but alive.

The plane that spotted lifeboat 12 on September 25 was a flying boat belonging to the Sunderland Division 10 Squadron of the Royal Australian Air Force. Pilot W.H. Garing was patrolling for U-boats on the way home from escorting an inbound convoy to Britain. The lifeboat was so small in the vastness of the ocean that they easily could have been missed it—had it not been for Ken Sparks waving his shirt.

A c k n o w l e d g e m e n t s

An exhibit at the Imperial War Museum in London sparked my curiosity about the children on the *City of Benares*. I subsequently spent many happy hours in the museum's research rooms, and deeply appreciated being able to use their extensive archive collection.

The excellent books and web sites that formed the basis for my research are listed at the end of this acknowledgement.

There are several songs quoted in the text. I am very grateful to the lyricists from days gone by—their words beautifully capture the poignancy of the time.

Run, Rabbit, Run, by Noel Gay 1939

All Things Bright and Beautiful, by Cecil Alexander 1848

Roll out the Barrel (Beer Barrel Polka), English words by Lew Brown and Wladimir Timm 1939

Spanish Ladies, an 18th century traditional sea song

There's Always be an England, by Ross Parker and Hugh Charles 1939

Rule Britannia, words by James Thomson, music by Thomas Arne 1740

Pack Up Your Troubles, by George Henry Powell and Felix Powell 1915

Excerpts from "Bulldog Drummond" by Sapper (Herman Cyril Mac Neile), originally published by Hasell, Watson, and Viney Ltd. in 1920, are now in public domain.

I've drawn on the memories and sensibilities of a number of English friends and family. A huge debt of gratitude goes to Peta Lunberg and Bryan Adams, who provided many insights into wartime life and English childhood. They also put me up (and put up with me!) while I wrote the first draft of the book, a kindness that changed my life. I am deeply grateful to Geoffrey Greet, survivor of the sinking of the *SS Laconia* in 1942, who helped with nautical terms and offered a unique perspective on surviving a torpedo attack. Fred Forrest, Mary Harrison, the Liverpool History Society, and Keith Hodgson all provided much needed additional information on war-torn Liverpool. Thanks also go to Jennifer Wilson, Diana Roach, and Wendy Wynne-Jones who helped with personal details about English childhood; to Victor Hodgson for background on Scottish ports; to Pat Dacey, for reading the manuscript with her astute English eyes; to Alia Hogben for information about turbans; and to Carol Harrison for her meticulous attention as copy editor.

I never would have been brave enough to write a novel had it not been for the initial encouragement of Shelley Tanaka and the example of my remarkable mother, writer Laurie Lewis.

The book came alive from the moment that Peter Carver shared his keen editor's eye. It would not have seen the light of day, had it not been for his guidance, sage advice, wit, and good humour.

Every day I am thankful for the support and wisdom of my husband, Tim Wynne-Jones. For forty years he has been my best friend, confidant, and advocate. Our grown children Xan, Maddy, and Lewis are constant sources of inspiration to us both. I am grateful for each moment of our shared lives.

Recommended Readings

There are a number of good books about the *City of Benares* disaster that I have used for my research. Here are some suggestions if you would like to find out more:

Barker, Ralph. *Children of the Benares: A War Crime and Its Victims*. Liverpool: Avid Publishers, 2003.

Huxley, Elspeth. *Atlantic Ordeal: The Story of Mary Cornish*. New York: Harper & Brothers, 1942

Mann, Jessica. *Out of Harm's Way: The Wartime Evacuation of Children from Britain*. London: Headline Book Publishing, 2006

Menzies, Janet. *Children of the Doomed Voyage*. Chichester, UK: John Wiley & Sons, 2005.

Nagorski, Tom. *Miracles on the Water: The Heroic Survivors of a World War II U-Boat Attack*. New York: Hyperion, 2007.

Smith, Lyn. *Young Voices*, Viking, 2007

Summers, Julie. *When the Children Came Home: Stories from Wartime Evacuees.* London: Simon & Schuster, 2011

Excellent websites include:

The Imperial War Museum:
http://www.iwm.org.uk/collections/item/object/80020747

The BBC's WW2 People's War:
http://www.bbc.co.uk/history/ww2peopleswar/stories/80/a6192380.shtml

Mackenzie J Gregory's Ahoy—Mac's Web Log:
Naval, Maritime, Australian History and More: http://ahoy.tk-jk.net/Letters/PicturesoftheSSCityofBena.html

The Wartime Memories Project:
http://www.wartimememories.co.uk/ships/cityofbenares.html

Uboat.net: http://uboat.net/allies/merchants/crews/ship532.html

Liverpool Blitz at 70:
http://www.liverpoolblitz70.co.uk/tag/city-of-benares/

Collective Worship Resource, Bess's speech on forgiveness: http://cowo.culham.ac.uk/assemblies/011s_forgiving.php

Photo credit: Matt Miller

Interview with Amanda West Lewis

What was it like to stumble on a piece of history that most people today are unaware of? What drew you to wanting to tell the story for young readers?

In 2011, I saw an exhibit called "The Children's War" at the Imperial War Museum in London, England. In it, there was this amazing photograph of five boys wearing oversized sailor's caps, with huge smiles on their faces. I read the caption. It said something like "Children Back from the Dead." It went on to explain how the boys had survived for eight days in a lifeboat after being torpedoed in the middle of the Atlantic. I looked at the boys again. They were so excited. They looked like they had been on the best adventure of their lives. I wanted to find out about their story, and what they'd lived through on the lifeboat.

This could be seen as a terribly sad story, or a magnificently inspiring one. Which do you think it is and why?

This is a terribly sad story *and* a magnificently inspiring one. I went through huge waves of sorrow as I was writing. I spent days writing and weeping. At one point I wondered if I would have to abandon the book because it was just too sad. But as I learned more about the children, they became alive to me. They weren't just numbers, but individual lives with interesting histories. Eighty children died. It was an unspeakable tragedy. Yet by writing about them, I suddenly felt as though they were alive again.

I started to see the world through their eyes. They were incredibly inspiring. The children had a common belief that they were part of a larger story—the story of winning a terrible war. I was really moved by their sense that they were doing something as part of a greater good. I was deeply impressed by their bravery and selflessness. I wanted to write about hope and survival.

I still wept as I wrote, but I felt as though the children on the *Benares* were having a chance to speak, and to be remembered. I wanted to honour them by telling their story.

While the CORB children group suffered the largest percentage of losses, one hundred lascars also were lost in the sinking of *The City of Benares*. For the most part, the lascars remained a mystery to the children. Why was that?

It was a very different time. The whole idea of a group of people coming from another country and dedicating their lives to particular jobs is really foreign to us. The word "lascar" comes from a combination of Persian and Arabic words meaning "the army." It refers to sailors and militiamen from India who were hired to serve on British ships. Lascars were liked because they were good at their jobs, courteous and, most importantly, worked for a quarter of the money paid to European sailors.

With the advent of the war, over 40,000 lascars were hired to work on merchant ships. The lascars on the *Benares* had travelled with the ship when she was a luxury liner and they stayed on when the ship was requisitioned by the British Navy. Their jobs ranged from scrubbing the deck and working in the engine room, to serving at meals. Their pay was doubled, although it was still far below that of the British sailors.

In the 1940s, most people in England were raised to see their country as superior to others. People from other countries, especially those with darker skin, were often treated as inferior. Lascars were considered as "charming and childlike," but definitely inferior. The common wisdom was that it was important to treat them nicely because they would respond to kindness, work hard, and happily carry out their tasks. But for the most part they were not thought of as individuals.

They were expected to keep to themselves. Few spoke English. Since the escorts and crew didn't really see them as individuals, the children didn't pay much attention to them. There were a few exceptions, of course. Ramjam Buxoo, because of his rank and nature, was well respected. By all accounts he was an essential person for the survival of everyone on lifeboat 12.

There are puzzles that remain after you read this extraordinary story. For example, how do you think it was that the rescuers from the *Hurricane* didn't realize that Lifeboat 12 and its passengers had still not been accounted for?

You have to understand the scale of what the *Hurricane* was doing. They had raced over 300 miles to get to the site, working through the night without sleep, pushing the ship's engines to their limit. The *Benares* had sunk eighteen hours before, in a huge storm, with changing currents and winds. When it went down, it sent up a thirty foot wave, pushing water, boats, rafts, and debris up and out in every direction.

Lieutenant Commander Simms from the *Hurricane* made a plan based on common naval practice. He gathered information about the prevailing winds and decided to start his search thirty miles east-northeast of where the *Benares* had gone down. This, he calculated, would be as far as the winds could have carried any lifeboats by the time they arrived. From there, the *Hurricane* began a "box search." They sailed twenty miles due west, then turned and went one mile due south. They turned again then went back twenty miles east and so on going one mile over, then twenty miles across. Every available crew member stood on deck with binoculars, searching, straining their eyes to look across the water as the ship moved as slowly as possible through the water.

It took them a long time to find the first lifeboat. It was much farther into the box than they had estimated. The boats hadn't travelled as far away from the disaster site as Simms had predicted, because they were waterlogged and heavy. The first boat that they found was the lighter lifeboat from the *Marina*. The other lifeboats and debris were found close to the original site of the disaster.

The only other boat that was not completely waterlogged, and was therefore lighter, was lifeboat 12. It was the only boat to have launched properly, and the only boat that made good use of the Fleming gears when the *Benares* went down. As a consequence, it had travelled farther than any of the other boats. It was well outside of the twenty-mile box search area.

Some people have suggested that Lieutenant Commander Simms confused the *Marina's* boat for one of the lifeboats from the *Benares*. He knew that there were twelve lifeboats on the *Benares* and he may have thought that he found all twelve boats, not knowing that one was from the *Marina*. I think it more likely that he searched until they completed their twenty-mile box search. They had combed through the area carefully, going through every inch in which they could expect to find boats or debris. It was too dark to search any more. They needed to get the survivors back to shore.

As it turned out, two of the three boys who died after being rescued by the Hurricane were children who appear in your story. Why did you decide not to reveal their identities in the story as you told it?

The three boys who died on the ship were Derek Carr, Terrence Holmes, and Alan Capel.

Derek Carr was not a boy whom I had named in the story, and I thought that mentioning his name might be confusing at this point, since we already had two other Dereks. Terrence was a boy from Wembley who I brought into the story as Terry, a friend of Ken's. I have no idea if they actually knew each other, but with both being from Wembley I thought it fair that they could be friends in the story. Alan Capel was Derek Capel's little brother.

Sonia was the only narrative voice in my story who might have been at the burial at sea. She wouldn't have known any of these boys so I didn't think the reader should hear about them from her. The two children in the story to whom these names would have meant anything were Ken Sparks and Derek Capel in lifeboat 12. When they got to Scotland they were told that there were only seven survivors from the CORB program. They weren't told any other details.

In fact, Derek Capel didn't learn about his brother dying on the *Hurricane* and being buried at sea until he heard about it at a reunion in 2000, sixty years after the fact. He had assumed his brother had drowned at the site of the *Benares* sinking. His family had never been told otherwise.

Can you say a little more about how this disaster affected the people who survived—especially the children? Did they keep in touch with each other in the years after the torpedoing?

The boys in lifeboat 12 stayed in close touch with each other. They also kept in touch with Father Sullivan, who lived to be 98 years old, and died in 2007, and Mary Cornish, who died in 1964.

The survivors handled their experience in different ways.

Derek Capel said that he was never able to hug anyone again after losing his brother Alan. He, Billy Short, and Johnny Baker knew that they were not to blame, but they never got over the loss of their brothers. They suffered what is called "survivor's guilt" all their lives. Colin said his mother had told him to just forget all about it. But he didn't, and he spent his life talking to children about the tragedy of war and the importance of facing things "head-on." Paul believed that every day of his life was a gift. Sonia, Derek, and Barbara thought that dealing with the tragedy might have been a bit easier for them—they could remember together, as a family. In fact, Sonia loved the sea. In 1953 she travelled by boat from Liverpool to Canada, where she taught at a girls' school for three years.

In 1988, Blake Simms, the son of Lieutenant Commodore Simms of the rescue ship HMS *Hurricane* organized the first official reunion of *Benares* survivors. Over the next twelve years, there were three memorials. The last was in 2000, at a special service in the Church of the Ascension in Wembley.

Bess and Beth were both very active in keeping the group in touch. They thought they should do all they could to keep the memory of the lost children alive. Beth organized the memorial in 2000 as a dedication to the children who died and Derek Capel read out all of their names during the service.

Of the thirteen seavacuees who survived, ten were at that

service. All of the boys in lifeboat 12 were there except for Howard, who had unfortunately died in a car accident in 1969. Bess and Beth were there, but Louis had died of a heart attack in 1985, when he was 56. Most of the paying passengers were there, including Sonia, Derek, Barbara, and Colin. Albert Gorman, the man who had pried Bess and Beth from the lifeboat, was there. Notably, Tommy Milligan, the sailor who saved Sonia, didn't go. He was profoundly affected by what had happened that night, and didn't want to experience any of it again.

Bess spoke passionately at the service in 2000 about trying to forgive the Germans who had torpedoed their ship. She believed that forgiveness could help to heal the wounds.

In an effort at reconciliation, two of the radio operators from the U-boat were invited. While not all of the survivors were comfortable with their presence, others, including Bess and Beth, made an effort to hear the story from their side.

For all of them, September 17 was always a day to remember the children who did not come home.

Often, when an author is writing about real historical events, she can get so caught up in the research that the need to tell a clear story is set to one side. How did you avoid this trap?

At first, I didn't avoid it! I love doing research. My first draft was heavy with research and, as a consequence, not a good story. I realized I had to narrow my perspective and make the story personal. I had to permit myself to imagine scenes that no amount of research could fill in. I had to make the story my own.

I thought a lot about memory. While the facts of the disaster are clear, the memories of the survivors are built upon years of telling and re-telling the story. Memories are not facts. They are always an interpretation of events. So I felt comfortable using bits of memories and fictionalizing them so that I could bring everything together into a cohesive narrative.

Even then, I still found it hard to set aside the research. It seemed that every day I would find some new tidbit I wanted to include. But I would ask myself, "Does this further the story, give detail to the character, and enrich the setting? Or am I just showing off more information?" I had to keep my research out of the way of telling the story.

In the end, I had to accept that there are hundreds of different ways of telling this story. I could only do one, so I had to make choices. What I have written is my version, which is very much a fiction.

This is your first historical novel for young readers— though you have written a number of other books for this audience. What advice do you have for young writers who

might want to write their own stories based on historical events?

Historical events can be seen from many different perspectives. I think the first thing is to try and see an event from all sides. Get up close and see details. Back up and take a long view. Look at it from the point of view of a pet cat, a journalist, an old man remembering his youth. Try it in the voice of someone on the outside, someone not connected to the story. Find out which perspective will work for your re-telling of the event.

I think it is important to play. I have spent a lot of my life doing theatre. In theatre you find out about characters through improvisation. So in writing a story, I put my characters together and let them improvise. I listen to their dialogue. I watch their actions. I observe their emotional state and the inflection in their voices. I pay attention to their timing, to pauses, to the turn of a head. I spend time in the room with them, taking on different roles. I laugh when they laugh and cry when they cry.

Play. Listen. Observe. Fall in love with your characters. Write a story that matters.

Why did you decide that you wanted a portion of the proceeds from this book to go to the charity, Save the Children?

The story in this book belongs to the children who were on the *SS City of Benares*. I think that the children would want some good to come from their tragedy. I wanted to try and find a way for their story to make a difference to other children's lives.

Save the Children ensures that the health, education and rights of children are protected worldwide. By donating to Save the Children we can all help children, especially those in war-torn countries and in poverty, to better lives. I think that the children on the *SS City of Benares* would approve of the Save the Children vision and mandate:

> Save the Children is the world's leading independent organization for children, delivering programs and improving children's lives in approximately 120 countries globally. We save children's lives. We fight for their rights. We help them fill potential.

> OUR VISION is a world where every child attains the right to survival, protection, development, and participation.
> OUR MISSION is to inspire breakthroughs in the way the world treats children, and to achieve immediate and lasting change in their lives.

> Across all of our work, we pursue several core

values: accountability, ambition, collaboration, creativity, and integrity.

Thank you for your thoughtful answers, Amanda—and for your story of this event.

For more information, go to www.savethechildren.ca